A TROPICAL FRONTIER

A Tropical Frontier, by Tim Robinson

MILTON'S BIG NIGHT OUT

A Bad Dog Book

TIM ROBINSON

Port Sun Publishing
PORT SALERNO, FLORIDA

ISBN: 9798429703992

Printed and bound in the USA.

Cover design, Patrick Robinson

To Sheila Katz. You insisted, so here you go.

Milton's Big Night Out

(Based on true events)

Sniff! Sniff!

Oh, boy! A rabbit!

The big brown dog burrowed his thick, black snout into the pine needles for a better impression of the scent. Then he bounded off, down the trail.

It was an extensive forest of longleaf pine, open and easily traversed except for occasional patches of saw palmetto. Buddy didn't like saw palmetto. It was scratchy, and sometimes the spines on the branches poked him in the eyes or his nose and made him sneeze. Saw palmetto was an excellent place for rabbits to hide, but Buddy was good at making rabbits think he was coming right in there to get them. They would get scared and run away – and the chase was on!

One hundred and sixty acres isn't that much for a dog like Buddy.

"BUDDY BOY! HERE, BOY!!"

Buddy's ears perked. He looked towards the direction the scent led. Then he sighed and headed in the general direction of home, but not before taking another whiff, to simply enjoy the aroma and cement it to memory. He had chased this particular rabbit before. Of course, after all these years, he had chased nearly every rabbit in the entire one hundred-sixty acres – The Last Resort, it was called.

One hundred and sixty acres isn't that much for a dog like Buddy.

"BUDDY BOY! HERE, BOY!!"

He trotted along the lakeshore – taking care for moccasins – and around the cypress stand that grew along the north shore of the lake. He stopped there, as he always did, to sniff at the place where Pappy shot that giant, marauding bear several years back. Then he headed in the general direction of the fence line, keeping his thick, black snout to the ground.

Suddenly, he stopped. He sniffed at the air, then dashed several paces to another place where he investigated a new scent.

What's this?

The hairs on his back bristled. His ears lay flat.

He lifted his head to scan the surrounding area, and his floppy ears perked. He listened.

There were coyotes around. That was one of Okey Donkey's jobs, to keep them off the property – but this wasn't coyotes. There were bears too. That was one of Buddy's jobs, to keep them away. There were even panthers and bobcats. And opossums and armadillos! And those "Dad-gummed Ra-coons!" as Pappy called them

But this was none of those things. This was a much more insidious and vile intruder, this one – or these ones. They traveled in a pack, so the scent was that much more vexing, bedeviling, and yes, even tantalizing, for it was part of Buddy's make-up, born of generations, to make sure that no one and nothing set foot on his one hundred and sixty acres without his knowledge and express permission. No, this enemy was much more cunning, treacherous, and guileful than any old bear or panther or raccoon. This enemy was most dangerous because they always traveled as one and were known around here, at least by Grandpappy, as "Them Durn-testable Neighbor Dogs!"

Yes, Buddy took his job seriously. From the first time he had heard Pappy utter those words, when he was still a puppy, Buddy had taken it upon himself, as job one, to keep their one hundred and sixty acres clear of Them Durn-testable Neighbor Dogs!

"BUDDY!! COME ON!! LET'S GO!!!"

Oh, yeah. I forgot.

Buddy looked around once more, his mind ablaze that the insubordinate invaders had been here without his knowledge. With neck hairs bristling, he started home along the fence line. He turned the corner at the big, green barn, then followed along the grassy lane towards the farmhouse. Okey Donkey came out to greet him.

Buddy got along fine with "Oke," as they called him, because they were on the same side. It was their job to keep the place free of varmints. But it still struck in his craw that Oke had killed a coyote once that had gotten into the pasture. Even now, all these years later, he could hardly look at Oke without hearing Pappy's words ringing in his ears: "Now, will ya look at that, Buddy? Old Oke brought me home a coyote!"

Yes, it would be good to bring a coyote home, like Oke had done; but in Buddy's mind, it would be better to bring those six Durn-testable Neighbor Dogs home and haul them right up onto the porch for Pappy. It never occurred to Buddy how difficult hauling six dogs, all at the same time, might be.

He stopped to sniff at Oke on the other side of the fence. Oke sniffed back, snorted, and walked along with him along the fence line. Small talk; Oke was good at that.

"BUDDY!! COME!! BAD DOG!!!!"

Oke gave Buddy the look.

Whoops, better get going!

4

Buddy picked up his pace and was almost there, trotting along the fence line, when in front of him a rabbit darted across his path; and under the split rail fence it went, and into the orange grove.

Every muscle in Buddy's body twitched, but he just watched after the rascally rabbit, like a good boy. He'd just have to let him go – except Buddy had an extremely short attention span, at least when it came to rabbits. And all of a sudden, he squeezed under the bottom fence rail, darted after the rabbit, and bounded off into the grove.

"I SAW YOU, BUDDY!! COME!! BAD DOG!!"

* * *

Okey Donkey was not just any donkey, but a miniature, as some people called him. He called himself compact and efficient. Grandma, the lady of the manor, had said so herself, that he was "efficient at storing up energy." For what use, no one could guess.

Yes, Okey Donkey was fat. He had heard all the "ass" jokes and comments, from people and other animals alike, about his girth. They said he looked like a bowling ball with legs, or a battleship when he approached from the front, and teased that he might take out the fence posts one of these days trying to make it through the stall gate.

But he didn't care. He liked it that way – compact and efficient. One of these days he might need all that stored up energy, and when he did, he'd be ready.

Oke was in charge of the pasture.

Of course, Star thought he was in charge. Star was the giant, inefficient, thoroughbred horse who shared the pasture with Oke and was his best friend in the world except for maybe Grandma or little Annie, the youngest granddaughter. Yet, if that were true, why was it the big horse ran for cover whenever danger reared its ugly head, while Oke challenged it head on?

Oke had chased the Durn-testable Neighbor Dogs out of the pasture many times. He'd even gotten in a good kick or near-stomp on more than a few occasions. All the animals knew for miles around that Okey Donkey's pasture was off limits, ever since the coyote incident. Of course, that had not played out exactly as everyone assumed it had. It was true, Oke had been in the process of chasing the coyote off the property at the time, but before Oke could get to it, the coyote had looked around to see if Oke was catching up and had run right into the big oak tree in the pasture and apparently broken its neck.

When Oke had brought it back, not mentioning the exact circumstances, of course, everyone from cackling hens to Lucy the milk cow to Grandma and Pappy to the kids and all the many and assorted aunts and uncles had hailed him as a hero. In fact, Oke had heard it had been printed up in newspapers as far away as Orlando: "Fat Little Donkey Wreaks Havoc on Coyote Population!"

Yes, this, the pasture, was Okey Donkey's realm, and no one entered without his knowledge and explicit permission. That went for Buddy as well. But that was not a point of contention, at least at this time, for it had been agreed upon long ago.

Both dog and donk understood that it was best this way, to work in unison.

As a gesture of good will, Oke did not say anything whenever Buddy snuck into the stalls to munch on Star's poop, which Oke thought disgusting. Apparently, it was a thing with dogs. Pappy said it was no big deal, that if he had to, like during the Great Societal Collapse, he'd eat horse manure too. He said they'd make fine meatballs for his spaghetti sauce.

Uncle Amos said that Oke's poop looked like "Giant Milk Duds."

Sometimes, Oke wondered about Uncle Amos. He was Pappy's brother and lived in the house attached to the barn.

Oke wondered about Pappy too.

He could see him over there in his "hot bathtub" – a cast iron bathtub set up on blocks with a firepit underneath.

Oke always wondered if what Aunt Mary said was true.

"One of these days, he's gonna drink too much, and we're gonna go out there the next morning to find a pot of boiled Pappy."

Oke wouldn't like that.

He liked Pappy. Not for any special reason, other than his long, gray beard. Pappy never did anything like feed him or fill his water or curry him or brush him. No, he didn't do anything except let him out in the morning, but that was enough for Oke. Pappy never locked him up, like others did, like when it was time to eat or come in at night. Of course, that was because Pappy never fed him or brought him in at night, but Oke didn't see it that way.

He was like that – short-sighted, as Pappy would say.

Oke believed Pappy, that he was short-sighted; but that did nothing to stop Oke from being short-sighted.

The most glaring evidence of this undesirable trait would come to light whenever Oke might escape his bonds, his prison, his kingdom – the pasture – and run free.

Yes! FREEDOM!!

Okey Donkey was especially adept at finding the right moment to dash out the stall door, or to find a weak spot in the fence and give it a good nudge, donkey style. Sometimes, he would work at a flimsy board for weeks or months until it finally gave way. Then he'd be off! It would be as if he had sprouted wings, and he would run and run and run!

But then someone would show up, one of the kids, or one of the many or varied aunts or uncles – but never Pappy.

Pappy would say, "Let 'im run! He was born free! He should live free!"

To which Grandma would say, "He wasn't born free, sweetie. He's a domestic animal."

Pappy would shrug, and Grandma would send everyone out with carrots in their hands.

Diabolical!

Okey Donkey knew he was short-sighted, but what else could he do? It was a carrot. It worked every time.

Oke watched as Buddy left and headed off towards the house. Aunt Doris had been out a minute ago, calling him again. But then Buddy sniffed at the air, altered course from the house, and dashed off into the orange grove.

"Mm-mm-mm," Oke mumbled under his breath. "Baaaad dog."

* * *

A bird in a gilded cage. That was what Grandma called Milton's world.

No one had known what he was the day he showed up. In fact, it had taken several months before Cousin Missy, from out of town, walked in one day, and said, "Why, that's a ferret!"

"A what?" everyone asked.

"Why," Cousin Eileen said, "I heard ferrets live out west. What's one doing way down here on the Florida prairie?!"

The question had never been answered, but others were.

"Why," Aunt Margaret said, "I heard they eat prairie dogs."

"Prairie dogs?!" the women, and Milton, had replied with revulsion.

Milton had no idea what a prairie dog was, but he was certain he did not wish to eat one. In his tiny brain, he had envisioned eating Buddy, because he was the only "prairie" dog he knew.

It had all started one day as Milton was traveling as part of a one-man circus wagon, going from one town to the next, traveling across the Florida prairie. He had escaped his cage and fallen off the wagon.

He had not been afraid, for it is not in the makeup of a ferret to be afraid – of anything!

Pappy said he was too stupid to be afraid.

Milton didn't care that Pappy said that, because he knew that Pappy was secretly afraid of him. He could tell by the way Pappy got up on his toes whenever Grandma let him run loose in the house, and how Pappy would rant and rave and shout, "Someone catch that thing b'fore I go for my shotgun!"

Milton knew Pappy would never go for his shotgun because Grandma wouldn't allow it.

They had found him out on the prairie, Uncle Dick and Cousin Tony, when they were on roundup. Cousin Tony's horse had almost stepped on him, and Milton had dashed around between the hooves, causing the horse, Pilgrim, to throw Cousin Tony off and run away. Cousin Tony had sprung to his feet and swore in colorful cowboy curses and pulled his six-shooter out and pointed it right at him. Milton, though, because he was fearless, had gone after him. Cousin Tony had backed away and called for Uncle Dick. Then they had stood around and discussed whether to shoot him for a varmint or take him home as a curiosity, all while staying well clear of him. Finally, they caught him, and – cursing in colorful cowboy terms because Milton had very sharp, pointy teeth – they had put him in a saddlebag and brought him home to Annie.

Milton loved Annie.

She was his little girl.

Yes, he had come to love it here. It was home. But it could be lonesome in the bedroom most all of every day. Sometimes, Annie would take him outside to the yard. He would run around and dance and sing and act like "a nutball," according to Pappy. Milton didn't care what Pappy thought. He liked running around like a nutball when he went outside. It was fun – and everyone laughed at him. All the other animals would gather around and watch, but none would come too close because they could see that he was fearless – or stupid.

Star, the giant race horse, would run away like a big baby if Milton so much as looked at him.

It could be lonely in his and Annie's bedroom when she was off at school.

He stared out the window. This was where Milton spent most of his time during the day, sleeping, rolled up on the window sill. He got up every now and then and looked out at the farm, at all the goings on. From his window, he could see Pappy's hot bathtub with the little firepit underneath. He could see the garden, the pasture, the big, green barn, the orange grove, and off in the distance, the lake. Beyond all that, there was the woods. He had never been to the woods. It looked dark and scary in there, but that didn't matter because he was a ferret – and fearless.

Yes, it was a comprehensive view from his window. From here, Milton could see everything that transpired on the back porch as well, though not that well because he was nearsighted. Milton didn't know he was nearsighted, even though Pappy stated with regularity that he must be "blind as a bat." He could see well enough to watch as one aunt or cousin after another came out and called for Buddy.

Milton liked Buddy all right. He wasn't in love with him, nothing like that, but he considered the big, brown dog all right.

"He's a good boy," everyone would say, and they would pat him on the head or scratch him behind the ears. Milton had also noticed, however, that they would often call him a bad boy.

"Bad dog," they would say.

That was usually when they would have to call and call for him because Grandma didn't want him going too far, or going over to mean old Farmer Perkins's property to fight with the neighbor dogs.

Milton kept watch for him. A few minutes later, he noticed the big, brown dog with the thick, black snout appear along the distant fence line. A minute later, Buddy stopped to talk to Okey Donkey. Then he started toward the house again, except a rabbit suddenly dashed out from under a bush. Although Buddy didn't take off after it right away, Milton knew exactly what would happen next. Sure enough, Buddy altered course, and off he went, under the fence and disappearing into the orange grove.

Milton shook his head.

"Bad dog," he mumbled.

Then he heard the door click, and he forgot all about Buddy.

Annie?!

It is! It is!

"Hi there, Milton!" she sang.

Milton's heart swelled. He loved Annie. She was his little girl.

Milton loved the way the afternoon sun coming in the window reflected off Annie's golden-brown hair. She set her books down, hurried over to the window, sat down in the chair next to it, and gave Milton a big, welcoming hug.

So? Are we going out?! Are we going out?!

Annie didn't answer. She set him down and changed her clothes.

"So, what do you want to do, Milton?" she asked. "I don't have much homework today."

I wanna go outside! I wanna go outside!

"How about if we go outside?" Annie said.

Sure! Let's go!

She swept him up in her hands and stuffed him in the big front pocket of her overalls.

"Now, stay right there, hear?"

Yep. Got it. Let's go.

Out into the hallway, around the corner, past the parlor.

Oh! Hey, Uncle Haskell! Hey there, Cousin Denny!

"Hey! It's Milton!"

In, through the swinging door, and:

9

Boy, does it smell good in here!

This was where it all happened, the center of all life in the big farmhouse along the prairie – the kitchen. It was an expansive kitchen, the biggest room in the house, with the southern windows looking out towards the orange grove, and the western ones toward the barn, the lake, and the woods.

There was always something doing in there, always lots of hands doing something, and lots of feet moving back and forth. Milton had learned long ago that it was a bad idea to run loose in the kitchen. Some of the aunts and cousins weren't that keen on small, rodent-looking animals with sharp teeth running amok at their feet. He'd been stomped on several times from fleeing feet, some wearing high heels, before he realized it was best not to have too much fun in the kitchen.

It was an oft told story of the time Aunt Janice stepped on him, and poop squirted right out his butt. The women had all laughed, and Milton had been horrified and humiliated.

He remained in his cozy, big, front pocket, his tiny, human-like paws holding on, nose and whiskers poking out, little beady eyes observing everything.

"No, Mother. You're supposed to whisk it, not stir it."

Grandma looked at her oldest, and said, "Sweetheart, I'm not sure if I know the difference, so … here you go." And she handed the implement over to Charlotte, who scowled.

Milton laughed.

Go get 'em, Grandma!

It was a big kitchen, and there was always a lot going on, sometimes several conversations at once. Milton had to decide whose might be the most interesting at any given moment.

Uncle Randy walked in, and that answered that question.

Milton liked Uncle Randy. He was always joking and funny. Grandma would sometimes get mad at him, and he would make a "Who? Me?" face. Then he would behave for a while.

"Mind if I sit down?" Uncle Randy asked, pulling a chair out from the table.

"Yes," several voices replied.

Uncle Randy sat down with plop and a grin.

Milton was aware that Uncle Randy was in the kitchen for the same thing he was.

Annie as well.

A few minutes later, the words arose from Aunt Charlotte, directed at Uncle Randy: "Out! Out, out, out! Here. Take these cookies and VAMOOSE!"

Annie and Milton looked to Aunt Charlotte to see if they were included in the banishment, then to Grandma, who smiled.

"Why don't you take Milton outside, sweetheart? Here," she said, picking out three – no four – cookies and handing them to Annie. "And here," she added, handing over some carrot tops. "Give these to Oke and Star. And would you call Buddy? He's been gone a good while now."

"Sure, Momma."

Once outside, Annie took Milton out of her big, front pocket, and said, "Four cookies, Milton. What do you think about that?"

I love it! Now gimme some!

Together, they sat on the back porch swing, munching on cookies and calling for Buddy.

"BUDDY! HERE BOY! COME ON, BUDDY!"

Annie looked down at Milton, and he up at her.

Together they sighed, "Bad dog."

Chapter Two

Darn it.

Yes, the rabbit got away.

Buddy performed the standard reconnaissance drill, trying to locate the scent again, but he had chased the rabbit into a dense stand of saw palmetto, which had disturbed a whole family of rabbits, and they had all dispersed in every direction.

In the old days, Buddy would have gone crazy trying to follow any or all of the trails all at once, but he had learned over the years to concentrate on one rabbit at a time. It was just that, although each rabbit had its own scent, after a while they all started mingling together and making it terribly difficult to discern one rabbit's trail from another's. So now there were half a dozen different trails he could follow, and Buddy was in the middle of considering which one to take, when something creaked inside his head. He scowled deeply.

He tried to remember.

Oh, yeah!

Someone had been calling.

Now, who was that?

It did indeed make a difference, who was calling.

Some voices he was more likely to come for, and others much less so. It depended on the time of day as well; that is, if it was time for breakfast or dinner or if Pappy was in the hot bathtub. Only the rarest of distractions could take precedence over Pappy in the hot bathtub.

Most of all, however, the voice that Buddy responded to with heartfelt glee, no matter the time of day, was that of Annie – his little girl.

There was nothing Buddy wouldn't do for Annie – any time, day or night, especially if it was getting-home-from-school time, which, in Buddy's mind, translated to the best time of day: snack time!

The cookies, cake, doughnuts, or whatever would not last long.

Buddy cocked a big, brown, floppy ear and listened. There it was.

"BUDDY BOY!!"

Oh, boy! Annie's home!

Buddy forgot all about "wascally wabbits," as Pappy called them. He dashed off in the direction of home: through the pine and palmetto forest, across the slough, around the end of the cypress swamp, under the fence, through the orange grove, and, finally, under the other fence by the grassy lane.

From here he could see her, in her usual spot, on the porch swing with Milton. Buddy dashed past Oke and Star – a polite nod – and down the grassy lane.

"Hi, Buddy!" Annie said as he ran up. "Hey, Milton! Look who's here! It's your old pal, Buddy!"

Buddy wagged furiously.

He gave Milton a polite but curt nod. He liked Milton all right. He wasn't crazy about him, of course. The little guy was scary with all those sharp, tiny teeth, and he smelled funny. This was not to mention Buddy might have been a little jealous of Milton because he got to live with Annie in her room and ride around in her big, front pocket. Buddy often wondered at how snug and cozy it must be inside Annie's big, front pocket and to be able to just go with her anywhere she went.

Sometimes, Buddy wished he was small, like Milton.

True, Buddy might have been a tad jealous of Milton, but if the little guy ever were to find himself in trouble, Buddy – though he wasn't really aware of it – would give his all to save him.

It is that way with dogs.

Especially, it was that way with Buddy.

This was his one hundred and sixty acres; he was sworn by birthright and the unwritten Canine Code of Honor to protect it and all that lay within it. That would include Milton – even Kitty for that matter.

Ugh.

Buddy barged ahead into the swing, pushing it backwards and making it squeak. He welcomed the scratch behind the ears – a one-handed one because Annie was holding Milton with the other one. Once Buddy had his full reassurance that Annie still loved him, he sat down and put on his best, cutest face.

"Awww," Annie said. "Do you want a treat too, Buddy?"

Are you kidding me?! I had a dozen rabbits on the line out there!

Buddy's eyes remained transfixed on Annie's hand as it reached down and into her pocket. He started drooling, excessively.

"Ew," Annie said, and she moved her knee out of range.

Buddy's eyes never left her hand.

"I saved some for you, Buddy," she said. She looked out towards the orange grove. "Where were you, anyway? It took forever for you to come."

I was chasing rabbits! I almost got one this time!

"Well, I'm glad you came home. You're a good dog, Buddy."

Annie handed him his treat. He gently took it from her hand, then swallowed it whole.

"Grandma's right," Annie giggled. "You didn't even taste it, did you?"

Oh, I tasted it. It was delicious. You got any more?

She did have another one. Buddy thoroughly enjoyed that one with equal dispatch.

They sat there a while, Annie petting Buddy and holding Milton, talking to them.

Then Cousin Shannon said through the open Dutch door, "Annie. Would you come over and get Buddy's dinner, please?"

Oh, boy!

Buddy paced frenziedly as Annie went to the Dutch door, which was closed on the bottom and open on the top, and took the bowl of food.

"Sit, Buddy," she said, and Buddy's butt hit the deck.

She bent over and dumped the food into his dog bowl, which Pappy had nailed to the porch. Buddy had a bad habit of getting hungry and walking off with his bowl in the hopes that he might find someone to fill it and then forgetting where he had left it.

"I'll pump you some new water too," Annie said.

She grabbed his water bucket and went over to the pitcher pump, out by the horse turnout next to Pappy's hot bathtub. A minute later, she came back with a fresh bucketful.

She set it down next to him, and said. "Okay, Buddy. Milton and I are going in now."

Buddy didn't really hear her. During this ten seconds of each day, a parade of neighbor dogs and wascally wabbits and uppity cats could sashay by, wearing tuxedos, pink tutus, and Viking cow-horn helmets, and Buddy would hardly notice.

When he finished his meal, Buddy looked around.

Hey! Where did everybody go?

*   *   *

Milton was glad to get back inside, especially since there were doings in the kitchen, which there almost always were. The problem was that there was always the chance that Annie would take him back to their room and leave him there.

Gratefully, this was not the case today.

Annie did indeed have homework, so Milton spent the next half hour trying to get Annie's attention, so they could play. After several attempts and multiple setbacks, Annie closed her book.

"All right, Milton. Let's see what's going on outside."

14

Oh, joy!

Milton proceeded to perform his best, most unbecoming, deranged-looking dance. Annie giggled and scooped him up and put him in her big, front pocket.

Back through the living room: "Hi, Uncle Moe! Hi, Cousin Terry! Hi, Cousin David!"

"Hi, Annie!" came the replies. Then, "Hey! It's MILTON!"

Through the big, swinging kitchen door they went.

Milton took a deep breath. The kitchen never smelled quite the same, but it was always magnificent.

Annie and Milton sat quietly in the chair by the window as the women – aunts, cousins, and Grandma – went about their chores of making the kitchen and whole house smell so good.

"Did Buddy eat all his dinner?" Grandma asked.

Annie and Milton shrugged.

"I don't know where he was off to today," Grandma said. "Did he look all right to you?"

"Sure," Annie replied.

Milton always wondered about Buddy, what he did when he was out there for so long. He liked Buddy all right, but he was a little jealous. And why wouldn't he be? Buddy got to come and go as much as he wanted, sometimes even at night. Grandma didn't like him going out at night, though, because she was worried he was getting old now.

On the other hand, Buddy was never allowed in the house when there were doings in the kitchen, which was almost all the time, whereas Milton, if he and Annie were very quiet and still, could sometimes stay for a long time, and maybe even get treats.

Milton had no difficulty with the quiet part, but the still part could be trying at times.

He looked out the Dutch door, open at the top and closed at the bottom. Buddy was out there right now, looking ridiculous, jumping up and down in front of the door, hoping someone might see him and let him in.

Milton had heard that back in the old days, Buddy would scratch at the door. He got in trouble for that, so he started barking, and he got in trouble for that too. Then he stopped barking and started howling, and that had been the worst, according to Grandma. The aunts and cousins would laugh and tell stories of Grandma chasing Buddy away by waving a broom at him out the Dutch door window. Milton thought that would have been a fun thing to see. Anyway, one day Buddy finally figured out that the only acceptable way to – possibly – get everyone's attention in the kitchen was to jump up and down in front of the half-door while looking in with a big, sad face.

It never worked. But there he'd be, every day, his giant head bobbing up and down. Every few seconds, there he'd be, his big brown face looking in: up, down … up, down; there, gone … there, gone.

Milton was getting bored. Sometimes he would just curl up in Annie's big, front pocket and take a nap, but he was too wound up today.

Buddy up … Buddy down. Buddy up … Buddy down.

Milton couldn't stand it any longer. He tried for an escape from the big, front pocket so he could get away and run around the floor and get things moving around here! But Annie was too fast, and she caught him.

"No, Milton!" she said, and both of them, Milton and Annie, froze.

They looked to Aunt Charlotte, who was glaring and scowling and didn't have to say the words. Slowly, Annie got to her feet and together, girl and ferret, they trudged out the door.

Buddy was happy about it anyway.

"So, what do you guys want to do?" Annie asked.

No one had a suggestion.

From the kitchen, "Did Buddy eat all his dinner?"

"Yes, ma'am!"

The trio walked out to the turnout and talked to Star and Oke, then down along the barn and checked in on the chickens. Milton found everything outside utterly fascinating, but for some reason he found chickens most interesting of all. Especially the eggs. He loved eggs. Cooked any way or not at all, he'd gobble them up. There were always eggs in there. Big, fat, juicy eggs!

Annie would sometimes set him down, and he would run over to the chicken-wire coop and dash up and down along its length, looking for a place to get in. Milton could get in some very small holes. Pappy still talked about the time Milton squeezed under the bedroom door. That was before Pappy had put something on the bottom of it so he couldn't do that anymore.

There were a few possible access points on the chicken coop, but Annie would always catch him before he had time to work out a definite plan of action.

They strolled along the grassy lane that separated farm from orange grove, then turned right and walked along the pasture fence in the direction of the lake. Milton loved going down to the lake and playing on the shore there. Sometimes, he would even go into the water. Annie would descend into a panic, of course, scoop him up, and tell him how dangerous that could be.

It was always the same thing with Annie, always worried about something. No matter where they were, there was always a warning: "Not in there, Milton! Star and Oke will flatten you like a pancake!" or "Not out in the open, Milton! That hawk will get you for sure!" or "Not in there, Milton! Those snakes and alligators will gobble you up in one bite!"

Milton didn't see the problem. He was fast. Real fast.

All the aunts and uncles and cousins said so.

Milton sighed. Sometimes he wished he was big, like Buddy.

Annie scooped him back up, and they watched as the big dog went for a swim.

Oh! And an alligator can't get Buddy?!

"Don't go too far out, Buddy," Annie warned.

Milton scowled.

A minute later, as if they all heard it at the same time, they looked to each other, then down the meadow towards the grassy lane. They watched, and there it was: Big Red, Pappy's old, cranky pickup truck.

"Mr. Ford's crowning achievement," as Pappy put it.

They watched as it clunked along, then as he saw them and waved out the window, then as the clanky truck passed around the corner of the pasture fence.

Buddy was out quickly, pausing long enough to shake water all over Milton and Annie. Then off he dashed, down and around the fence line towards home.

Chapter Three

Pappy claimed it as his own pinnacle of achievement.

He called it his hot bathtub; because it was a bathtub that was hot. He had come up with the idea years earlier as he had been soaking in his tub in the bathroom. He'd sit in there for hours sometimes, reading his encyclopedias. There was some discussion among all the aunts, uncles, and cousins as to whether he was really reading the encyclopedias, but it was generally accepted that he read at least half of them. That was because approximately half of his facts proved correct under later recall.

Regardless, it had hit him one day as he sat in his regular bathtub, staring out the window, that wouldn't it be nice if he could take a bath outside, so he could enjoy his world and his day, and sometimes late into the night too?

He had gotten the tub, resale, down at Cousin Travis's resale shop. With pride, he and Buddy had driven through the streets of town with his new tub in the back of Big Red. Of course, Buddy always enjoyed a jaunt into town, or any occasion that might present itself for him to sit in Big Red and gaze out the windows and feel the wind puffing out his expansive cheeks like two, fuzzy, weather balloons. After making several passes down Main Street so everyone could see his prize, Pappy and Buddy had taken the tub home, set it up on blocks right next to the old pitcher pump in the yard, filled it with water, and proceeded to build a fire under it.

It had been an event. All the relatives had been there and even friends and acquaintances from town, all to see Pappy's new "Most Heavenly Contrivance," as he had dubbed it. All had gathered on the back porch that day to watch as he filled it with water, stoked the fire, tested the water temperature, and threatened to remove his skivvies. Then he buckled under pressure from Charlotte who threatened to come out there and turn him over in it if he did.

Nowadays, no one cared. It was old hat: Pappy's hot bathtub.

Regardless, all knew not to come around the back yard during hot bathtub hours for fear of catching him in the process of getting in or out. Yes, Pappy had prevailed, explaining that a person cannot take a proper bath with their skivvies on. Everyone, of course, had to agree, much to the chagrin of Charlotte, who fumed and threatened to that very day.

Pappy had little doubt that the day might come when he would indeed be tumbled from his tub, for he had raised a head-strong girl. In an effort to keep her fiery retribution at bay, he had rigged a flimsy curtain in front of the tub, just for getting in and out. Pappy was like that, resourceful and obliging.

All the boys down at the shop said so.

After a long, hard day on the job, with farm chores afterward, there was nothing Pappy liked better that reclining in his hot bathtub and enjoying his world and his day. He would sit there and read his encyclopedias or work on his novel or blow on his harmonica. He would drink beer and talk to Buddy, Oke, Star, the mockingbirds, anoles, and anyone else that might pass by until it was suppertime.

Today, the tub was extra hot from the heartwood he had used from the tree he had cut down just that morning.

Slowly, Pappy descended into the water.

"Ah … AH … AHH … … Ahhhhhhhhhhh!" Then a heartfelt "HOO!! That's goooood."

It took a minute, while he was lost to the world, then he settled in. He reached into his authentic, redwood cooler and pulled out a beer, popped it, and took a long, satisfying drink.

"Ahhhhhh! That's goooood."

Here, at this point, he would say, "The first drink is for thirst, the second for taste." Then he would finish with, "The third, fourth and beyond are for whimsy, mirth, and unbridled madness."

Leaning over the rail, he said, "Here ya go, Buddy," and he poured some beer, only a taste, into Buddy's beer bowl.

Buddy lapped it up.

"Nice out, ain't it?" Pappy said.

Sure is. And this beer is delicious!

Next to the tub, opposite Buddy's spot, was Pappy's table with his book, writing pad, and transistor radio.

Pappy scratched at his long, gray beard and looked off towards the barn. He scowled.

"I don't suppose I blame those two doves for bein' a might ticked at me." He sighed.

Pappy puffed out a few bars of "Oh, Susanna" on his harmonica, the only song he knew, then looked off towards the barn. He scowled.

Buddy looked at the two doves sitting on the barn roof, staring at the empty spot where the maple tree had been.

19

"How was I to know there was a nest up there?" Pappy grumbled. "Now I suppose they'll just sit there ever' night for the next week, waitin' for me to put their tree back. You know what I'm sayin', Buddy?"

I know what you're sayin'.

Pappy shifted in his tub so he couldn't see the doves glaring at him in his peripheral vision.

He leaned over and pushed some kindling under the tub with his "fire stick," then settled into *Vol. 9: Darwin, Charles to Eastern Religion.*

A little while later, Star and Oke ambled over. Star stuck his head over the fence to see if he could reach Pappy's straw hat, but Pappy had moved the tub to the other side of the pitcher pump years ago just for that reason.

Buddy gave them a nod.

Sorry, fellas. No beer for you.

Buddy wasn't above rubbing it in, especially with Star.

Star, the big, chestnut thoroughbred, thought he was something, just because he went to horse shows and won ribbons and the girls all fawned over him because he was so tall and beautiful and graceful and blah, blah, blah. And because he was so fast.

Still, Buddy thought today might be the day, the day he would win the race along the fence line.

Buddy thought Star on the dim side, actually.

Grandma and Annie came out the back door, and Buddy sprang to his feet. He looked to Pappy, who raised his beer in deference, then he dutifully took off after Grandma and Annie. It was feeding time for Oke and Star, one of the only things that could take precedence over Pappy in the hot bathtub and beer – and possibly Golden Flake Hot Potato Chips.

All the signs were there, all of them coming together.

Star's ears perked – dinnertime.

Oke's as well.

Buddy wasted none of that – time. He charged right up to the fence line, right in Star's face, and barked maniacally, as if he wished to get in there and chew Star's legs all the way down to nubs.

As usual, Star shook his head and ambled away, but then, as Buddy's plan took hold, the big horse could not resist the challenge and suddenly bolted towards the far end of the pasture. Buddy charged down the other side of the fence, bearing to the ground, getting everything he could out of his old body, barking madly. He had not quite caught up before Star turned around, snorted imperiously, and sprinted back down the fence line in the other direction, once again getting there some distance ahead of Buddy.

Oke didn't have time for all that. He was already in his stall, waiting to eat, when Star swaggered into his, a haughty smirk on his handsome face.

Oh, that smirk!

It drove Buddy crazy. He continued to run around insanely, around and around the barn and turnout, one way then the other like some mad dog.

Finally, he noticed Grandma, screaming at the top of her lungs, "BUDDY! NO!"

Oh. Sorry. I didn't hear you.

Grandma gave him a stern look. Then she gave him a tiny, very small, taste of horse feed.

Mission accomplished.

Buddy wandered back and forth as Grandma and Annie took care of all the horse stuff. He always wondered why horses took so much work.

Me? I'm easy. Feed me! Any chance you get!

When Star was finished with his grain and done dropping it on the barn floor for Buddy to gobble up, Buddy realized the fun was over. He headed back out to the hot bathtub to sit with Pappy.

Good old Pappy.

As Buddy approached, Pappy started singing the Buddy Boy song to what was playing on the transistor radio. The lyrics went kind of like this: *Oh, Buddy Boy, Buddy Boy. He's a good boy. He's Buddy Buddy Buddy boy*, and on and on. Then he would puff out a few bars of "Oh, Susanna" and sing "Buddy Boy, Buddy Boy" to that.

Buddy sat down with a big sigh.

"Did ya get those horses all squared away?" Pappy asked.

I suppose.

Pappy set his book down.

"Now, don't you fret about old Star, Buddy. He's fast, sure. And he looks good and all, with his fiery mane streaming behind, and his flowing tail seeming to dance along the fringes of the wind. But he ain't got nothin' on you and your big, giant, over-sized but well-formed head."

Pappy took a drink. He suddenly laughed, causing the bubbles to go up his nose.

"Aaaaa-chua-p-tooie!!" he choked, then, laughing and sputtering, he finally got the words out. "Did you see that fool horse today?! When I was cuttin' down that dead tree hangin' over the barn? Was that a hoot or what?!" Pappy snorted with glee. "Remember? That ladder come down with a bang, and Star took off like ... well, like his pants was on fire! Oh! Lord have mercy, but that was funny! Remember?! Me and you looked at old Oke, just standing there like nothin' happened, and all three of us gazin' off at Star, still running like ... uh –"

21

His pants was on fire?

"Exactly! Like his pants was on fire!"

Buddy imagined Star wearing pants, and they were on fire.

"Yep," Pappy concluded. "That Star, he's a bit high-strung, but he's all right."

I suppose.

A minute later, Pappy casually reached over to pat Buddy on the head, except Buddy lifted his head just as the fingers were coming down, and two of them went right into his nostrils.

"Dang it, Buddy! Why'd'ya always gotta do that?!"

Why do you always gotta do that?!

As Buddy blew his nose fitfully, Pappy rinsed his hand off. Then, while taking a moment to use his fire stick to push some kindling under the tub, something caught his eye.

"Will ya look at that, Buddy," he said with wonder. He sat up and squinted.

Buddy looked across the way, in the direction of the garden, windmill, and potting-shed, at the big bougainvillea bush.

"Is that what I think it is?" Pappy asked.

I think it is.

"Mm-mm," Pappy sighed. "I reckon that's why cats need nine lives. They can do some mighty stupid things. Imagine, Buddy? Would you ever try anything so stupid?!"

Not a chance.

They remained transfixed, watching Kitty, who was attempting to climb upward, into the incredibly, inconceivably thorny branches of a bougainvillea bush. It was obviously an attempt to get to the mockingbirds' nest there. The baby birds squawked in terror.

"She's good, though. Ya gotta give her that, don't ya, Buddy?"

I suppose.

"But nobody's stupid enough to try to climb a bougainvillea bush. Are they, Buddy?"

I suppose there's at least one.

"Yep," Pappy opined. "I suppose you're right about that."

With that, man and dog watched, entranced, as Kitty – black and white and proud – took her sweet cat time. She was an amazing acrobat and contortionist, and so, so patient. Each individual step upward, into the morass of long, spiky thorns, was conceived, studied, and reviewed before ever attempting the next move, no matter how small that move might be.

"Holy mackerel, Buddy. She might actually make it."

Minutes passed as they watched, mesmerized. Meanwhile, the closer Kitty came to the nest, the more frantic the mommy and daddy mockingbirds became, swooping down all around, churring and rasping madly, even diving into the branches, only inches from where Kitty perched on her cold, predatory haunches.

"Holy cow, Buddy. She's almost there!"

It appeared that it might be so, but then Kitty made that one, fated, false move, and – *Oops!* She reacted and bumped into another thorn.

Ouch!!

And another. *OUCH!! ... OUCH!! ... OUCH!! OUCH!!! OUCH!!!!*

The next second, Kitty was sitting on the ground under the bushes, the mockingbirds zipping and swooping triumphantly overhead. She appeared to be without too much damage, mostly to her pride, it seemed. She looked over at Pappy and Buddy, unruffled dignity defined, and disinterestedly turned away to lick her wounds.

"I don't understand cats. Do you, Buddy?"

Not at all.

The two old friends went on to discuss the social and family turmoil among the local birds, mostly concerning the mockingbirds, who had been trying to get one, their oldest, out of the nest for weeks now. But he just kept coming back.

"Danged kids," Pappy grumbled. "Ya chase 'em out the front door, and they come in the back when ya ain't lookin'."

Ain't that the truth.

"Sure is," Pappy replied. "Ya ever seen such a stubborn bird, Buddy?'

Can't say I have.

"He's causin' all kinds of discontent with the jays and cardinals. They're all up in arms lately."

Yep. Mm-hm.

"Oh, look! They're both on the bird bath! The jay and the mockingbird! What do you think, Buddy? They gonna fight? I'm bettin' that big old jay's got some dander; but we've seen what the mockingbirds can do, even to that hawk that lives around here. And more than once!"

They watched as the mockingbird faced the larger, tougher-looking blue jay, who was turned sideways. Every few seconds, the mockingbird would make a feint, and the jay would start, but not fly away.

"Wonder what they're fussin' about?" Pappy queried.

I don't know. I can't really hear what they're saying from here.

"I can't either," Pappy replied.

The back door slammed. Buddy sat up.

Annie!

First thing, Buddy checked to see if Milton was with her. Then he reflexively looked to Annie's bedroom window, and there he was, all splayed against the glass, gazing out at them.

How undignified.

"Hi, Pappy. Hi, Buddy."

"What do you say, kiddo?" Pappy replied.

"Not much," Annie said. She sat on the old, crooked stool next to the tub and rested her hand on Buddy's head. "Uncle Amos took Cousin Davy's bicycle again because he left it parked in the barnyard."

"Mm," Pappy said. "I suppose that's what Davy gets. He knows how Uncle Amos can be."

"Crotchety," Annie said.

"Yep," Pappy affirmed, "a mean old, crotchety old man." Then he said, "Did I hear that Buddy was a bad dog today?"

Annie scowled. She leaned over and wrapped her arms around Buddy's big, giant, oversized head.

"He's not a bad dog."

"Not from what I heard," Pappy replied. "Grandma said he didn't come back most of the afternoon."

Together, they looked at Buddy.

Hey, I was busy! Protecting the property! It's one hundred and sixty acres!

Buddy wasn't bothered, all this talk about bad dogs and whatnot. He always knew that no matter how long he was gone, or what he did, or what condition he was in when he got home, Pappy would always say, in the end, "Good boy, Buddy."

And Grandma too. In the end.

In reality, no one was easier than Grandma.

Annie sat back on her little stool next to the tub and rubbed Buddy on his belly with her foot.

"So," she asked. "Does Buddy really talk to you, Pappy?"

"Of course," Pappy replied. "Doesn't he talk to you?"

Annie looked at Buddy, looking at her, and she said, "I suppose so." She sighed. "Cousin Mary Ann says fifteen minutes until dinner."

"Got it," Pappy said, looking at his watch on his pile of things. "Fifteen minutes from … … now."

Annie giggled and replied, "No. It's more like twelve or thirteen minutes by now."

It was their normal routine – Pappy and Annie.

"And Aunt Charlotte said that if you come through the kitchen wearing only a towel again she's gonna yank it off, and you'll have to run up to your bedroom buck naked!"

24

Pappy smirked, and replied, "Not sure who's gonna get the worst of that one, me or her."

The hawk flew over, kreeing pompously.

Buddy looked up.

Showoff.

"There he is," Pappy said. "Flyin' all high and mighty."

"Until he messes with the mockingbirds, huh, Pappy?"

"That's right, kiddo. I think we all know who rules the skies around here."

"We sure do."

"Except at night, of course," Pappy said. "That big old horned owl has it over everyone at night, even the mockingbirds."

"How do you know the owl's a he?" Annie asked.

Pappy appeared only momentarily perplexed.

"Did I say he? Why, by all the rules of nature and society and 10,000 years of civilization, I suppose the owl, bein' in charge like he is, must be a she."

Annie looked at Pappy curiously.

"He's a ... she?"

Pappy took on a studious countenance.

"Absolutely," he said. "I think he's a she."

Buddy stared.

Sometimes you two don't make a lick of sense.

Pappy and Annie laughed.

A few minutes later, Pappy was hurrying through the kitchen, wearing only a towel and that crafty, old, Pappy grin.

"I know I'm a late, Mammy, but me and Buddy was busy as a hen in a fox house out there."

"Quit calling her Mammy!" Charlotte said.

"All right," Pappy said, and he gave Grandma a kiss. "Sorry I'm late ... ... Woman," and he scurried past Charlotte, gripping his towel extra tight as he did.

"And quit calling her Woman!"

Chapter Four

Evening time at the Last Resort.

There were folks over, aunts, uncles, and cousins.

Sometimes, from out on the front porch, it seemed as if the house itself were laughing: big convulsive belly laughs, the walls expanding and contracting with each guffaw. Aunt Cackie's cackle rose far above the rest, leading them on, like a merry, deranged choir of lunatics. And if Uncle Kenny got to the piano, well, it could get downright rowdy in there – and without one single, solitary drop of alcohol.

Pappy and Uncle Amos were out on the front porch, sitting in the green, metal, clamshell chairs, smoking their pipes and drinking Falstaff beer, which wasn't that good, but it was difficult to find in Florida. It tasted better because of that.

"Loud tonight."

"Yep."

"Been kind'a dry lately."

"Mm-hm. Dry."

"Yep."

If they wanted to, they could sit without talking at all because they knew all of the other's stories by heart since they had each experienced them, and/or told them, and/or heard them, hundreds, possibly thousands, of times.

They talked anyway.

"Remember the time we was goin' down to –"

"Yep."

"Fun, huh?"

"Mm-hm."

"Annie says ya took Davy's bike again."

"Yep."

"Left it in the barnyard again?"

"Mm-hm."

"Danged kid."

"Yep."

"He's a good kid, though."

"Yep. Mm-hm."

Uncle Amos looked at his beer.

"Almost out of Falstaff."

"We'll order some more down at Uncle Moe's."

"Should'a told 'im while he was here tonight."

"Mm-hm."

"Lookee there. Looks like Buddy a'comin'."

"Good boy, Buddy!" Pappy said. Then, "What's that in his mouth? Is that another dad-blamed possum?"

"It do appear so."

Buddy ambled up to the porch. He ascended the steps slowly, his prize in his mouth. Buddy never knew what to expect. Sometimes they'd say, "Good dog!" but other times they'd say, "Bad dog!" He still couldn't figure it out.

Warily, he lay his catch at the altar that was Pappy's feet. The two men looked at the possum, then at Buddy.

Finally, Pappy said, "Good boy, Buddy ... I suppose. But you're just supposed to chase the possums away. You know how Grandma is, ever since that time she saw that family of possums and all the babies and all. Well, just try to remember to chase possums, not catch them. Rats okay, possums not."

Okay. Got it. Chase not catch. Rats okay, possums not.

"And don't bring the carcasses back," Pappy added. "Ya know?"

You sure?

"Yes, I'm sure," Pappy replied.

Buddy sat there and watched as Pappy and Uncle Amos discussed whether the possum was dead or just playing possum. Its mouth was open, teeth bared, eyes wide and glassy.

Of course, he's playing possum. He's a possum!

The front door opened, and Annie stuck her head out.

"We're having dessert now." She looked down, and said, "Hi, Buddy!"

Hi!

Pappy nodded at the possum.

"Looks like our great, large-headed hunter has bagged a prize."

Annie looked, and her face fell.

"Oh, no. You think it's still alive?"

Pappy shrugged. "Don't see any marks, just a slathery coating of Buddy spit."

Annie looked at Buddy, who sat for her and looked pitiful.

She said, "You're not supposed to catch possums, Buddy. You might accidentally kill them, and Grandma says they're too cute when they're babies."

Buddy was bracing for it, the "Bad Dog," but it never came.

Whew!

27

"We won't mention it to Grandma," Pappy said. "Unless she asks."

"Sure, Pappy." Annie sighed. She looked down at Buddy, all forlorn and lonesome-hearted, and said, "You want to come in, Buddy?"

SURE!

And Buddy was in. As he went in, he heard the two men considering the possum.

"Ya think it's alive?"

"It was the last time."

"Buddy tries to be gentle. But remember the time with the baby rabbits?"

"Oo. That wasn't pretty."

"He felt bad about it."

"Mm-hm."

The old timers sat like that, staring at the possum and drinking Falstaff, when the possum suddenly lifted its head and looked around.

"Well, lookee there," Pappy said, and he sat forward in his green, metal, clamshell chair. "I'd better scare him back to death so everyone can come out and see him playin' possum!"

With that, Pappy started waving his hands wildly, trying to scare the possum and get it to pretend to be dead some more, but the possum didn't seem to be afraid of Pappy. He just got up, looked around as if checking for any lurking, big-headed, black-snouted, brown dogs, then moseyed on down the steps and disappeared into the darkness.

"Well, I'll be darned."

"Yep. Me too."

"Me too," Buddy said, and the door closed behind him.

*   *   *

Nighttime at the Last Resort.

The light from a full moon shone in the window of the bedroom. The curtains fluttered in a gentle breeze. A little girl lay sleeping. In a small cage attached to the far wall, Milton slept, snoozing, having been all wound up from having riotous fun with Annie before bedtime.

Then Grandma's voice had said, from down the hallway, "Lights out now, children!"

And that was that.

Milton hated nighttime. Even though he was by nature a nocturnal creature, nothing ever happened at night, at least not in his world.

His world included his little cage and the utility room, to which the cage was attached through a hole in the wall. The utility room, with the big sink and the washing machine and the water heater, was Milton's nighttime world. And it was boring. He had his toys, of course, and all his stuff he had "acquired," all pushed back behind the washer and water heater, but those things were only fun for a while. Then they'd get boring too.

It was good that he got wound up, then got tired. It was better to sleep at night, like everyone else.

But it just wasn't natural. Not for a ferret.

*   *   *

Everyone was in bed except for Pappy and Grandma.

They were in the living room, in their chairs, watching their new television set.

Buddy yawned and sat up a little. He could sense it in the air. He knew it before Pappy even knew it, little signals flashing on and off in his brain. He sat up and stared at Pappy intently. He barked.

"All right," Pappy said. "Don't pee your pants. I suppose it's just about snack time anyway."

Snack time?! Snack time?!! Ya-hoooo!!!

"Settle down, Big Head. Just settle on down there." The two of them ambled off to the kitchen. "Ya want anything, Mammy?" Pappy called out to the living room.

"No thanks, Pap."

A few minutes later, the kitchen door opened and Grandma stepped in, letting some of the smoke out.

"Do you need any help?" she asked.

Pappy and Buddy froze in place as Grandma discerned what was going on: Pappy sticking a piece of cheese, a small one, into Buddy's mouth.

"You're not supposed to give him cheese, honey."

Pappy looked at Buddy, surprise on his face, and said, "Bad boy! You took that right out of my hand!"

Grandma looked at Buddy.

No I didn't! He gave it to me!

Grandma stared at them, Pappy leaning way over to make his sandwich because Buddy was standing between him and the counter.

"Wouldn't it be easier if he didn't stand right there while you're doing that?"

Pappy shrugged.

Buddy the same.

A few minutes later, Pappy was back in his chair, eating burnt popcorn with cheese on it and a peanut butter and jelly sandwich with milk.

"Hey, Mammy! What's takin' so long in there?!"

29

"I'm making tea," she answered through the door. "Waiting for the water to boil."

"Then come on in here and wait for it to boil."

The door opened, and she said, "As soon as I sit down, the water will boil."

"Then," Pappy replied, "sit down, so the water will boil."

Grandma made a crinkly face, but saw the wisdom. She came back in and sat down in her matching chair. She got comfortable.

Tooooooooooot!

As Grandma got up, Pappy looked to Buddy.

"See? Works every time."

Buddy was impressed, but then, he was always impressed with Pappy. It was clear and patently obvious that he was the smartest and wisest person around. Pappy had told him so, in fact.

Later on, Grandma had gone off to bed, and Pappy was closing up, checking the doors, the lights, and he and Buddy went out to take care of business one last time.

"Ahhhhhhhh."

Ahhhhhhhh.

"Nice out, eh, Buddy?"

Yep. Real nice. And I think I smell rabbits.

"It's a little late for rabbits, don't you think?"

Well, they've been here; that's all I'm saying.

"Wascally wabbits."

Yeah. Wascally wabbits.

The moon was bright, but there were intermittent clouds.

They stopped at the pitcher pump, and Pappy gave his face a good dunking.

"Dang it. No towel."

They headed back to the porch, Pappy grouching at himself. When they got there, he reached for the towel that was supposed to be hanging there.

"Dang it. Wait right here, Buddy," he said, and he went into the utility room. The light went on. It went off. Pappy pulled the door behind him.

"That's better," he said. He tossed the towel where it didn't belong and started into the house. "Come on, Buddy."

The door. Hey, Pap. The door to the utility room's not closed.

"Come on, Buddy! Let's go! Bugs are gettin' in!"

But the door! It's not closed!

"Come on, Buddy!!"

Buddy looked at the door. It wasn't really open. It just wasn't really closed either.

"BUDDY! LET'S GO!"

Buddy sighed, then he followed Pap into the house.

Chapter Five

Milton was curled in a ball behind the washing machine.

It was a wonder world here, a bundly, snuggly place with all his favorite, softest, most best-smelling things: Milton's treasure trove. It was handy, being right in the place that all the laundry passed through. There were all kinds of good things, mostly socks, some with matches, others not. There were other articles, from shirts to blouses, a skirt or two, and even a whole dress. It had taken Milton a good amount of work to get that one back here, but not as much work as that pair of Pappy's overalls, which still had something in the pocket that Milton used to scratch himself behind the ears with. He assumed it was Pappy's old pocket knife, the one he regularly walked around and mumbled about losing, the one his grandpappy had given him. Milton had considered telling Pappy where it was, but up until now he had remained mum.

Yes, there was a whole sampling of the family and house in his snuggly, huggly place, from assorted clothing to dishrags, hand towels, and cloth napkins – one of Milton's favorites. Best of all, there was the place where Milton most liked to lay his head at night, Annie's pillowcase.

Nothin' better.

Then there was Pappy's underwear.

Milton kept those off to the side, just in case. He used them to wake himself up, if need be. As everyone knows, ferrets are slow waker-uppers, and a stiff shot of old Pap got him going every time.

He rolled over onto his back and stretched, his human-like hands and tiny fingers reaching in all directions. His little, pointy mouth opened in a cavernous yawn, exposing rows of tiny, sharp, white teeth. His beady eyes scrunched purposefully.

Sitting up, he looked around. Something was different. He could sense it. Everyone knows that ferrets have advanced senses and intuitions. He could feel it, the outside air, and the strange faint light in the room. Yes, something was different. His senses worked in harmony, awakening his brain, making him alert. He sat up higher and listened, then scurried around the corner of the washing machine.

His primal senses aroused him and took firm hold. Coming around the end of the washer, his curiosity was sated.

Milton's heart leaped into his throat. He wasted no time in scampering over to the door. He rolled onto his side, leveraged himself against the door jamb, and used his tiny, human-like hands to open it, just enough to squiggle through.

He looked out. It was a moonlit night. The moon was almost full, nearly like daytime, and he could see everything clearly, especially with his "superior" ferret eyesight.

All was quiet. He sniffed at the air and scanned the area. To his left, down the porch, was Pappy's truck. Beyond was the orange grove and the grassy lane leading out to the prairie. To the right was the horse turnout and barn, and then Pappy's hot bathtub. Milton looked around the corner, down the hill, beyond the big bougainvillea bush, towards the garden, windmill, and potting shed. Beyond that was the cow pasture.

He looked up at the moon and edged out onto the porch.

It felt good, the cool night air, the smell of freedom. He took a deep breath.

Ahhhhhh!

He scampered along the edge of the porch and went down the four porch steps, tumbling head over feet as he did.

He sat back and took it all in.

Where to start?

The chicken coop loomed large.

He was thinking about that when a voice out of the darkness said, "Hey. Bub."

Milton knew who it was.

"Over here," the low, gravelly voice said.

It was Kitty. She was sitting in the shadows, smoking a cigarette – or giving the appearance of it anyway.

Kitty thought she was something, always sashaying around, going wherever she liked – in, out, whatever – giving Milton the old stink eye.

"How's it goin'?" Milton asked.

"Hmph," Kitty snorted. "I should be askin' you that. I was wonderin' what was takin' you so long. Pappy left the door open hours ago."

"Hours ago, huh?"

"That's right," Kitty curtly replied, eyeing the morsel that was Milton.

"So," Milton asked nervously, "what's going on?"

"You're lookin' at it, bub. Just loungin', takin' it easy, waitin' for one of those rotten, rat-faced rats to show its ugly face." She glanced at Milton with her haughty cat face, and added, "Present company excepted."

Milton nodded.

They'd had the discussion, the differences between rats and ferrets. Milton had explained that ferrets don't taste that good. Kitty had replied that rats didn't taste that good either, but that didn't detract from the fun of torturing them to death.

Milton never did like the way Kitty looked at him, but he wasn't worried. Kitty would be in big trouble if she ever tried anything. Anyway, Milton was ready. He could take care of himself. Ferrets were fearless. Everyone knew that.

"Well," Milton said, taking stock in himself, "I'll see you later."

"Where ya goin'?" Kitty asked.

Milton shrugged. "Just taking a stroll." And he headed off towards the grassy lane.

The grass here was high, and ferrets aren't the best stompers or bounders or trailblazers. Being reminded of this, Milton astutely altered course so that he could stay along the pasture fence where Oke and Star kept it nice and trimmed.

"What are you doin' out here," a gruff, curt voice asked.

"Oh, hey there, Oke. Star. How's it goin', fellas?"

"We're good," Oke replied, looking to Star, who remained back a few feet. "So, what are you doin' out here?"

Milton had a sudden urge to make a quick dash in and back, just enough to make Star jump, but he decided against it. He had seen what Star did to rats, of whom the giant horse was also afraid.

Milton didn't like the rats either. No one liked the rats, except for Bundy Mac, the yellow rat snake.

That was one Milton didn't want to run into tonight, Bundy Mac. He wasn't "officially" part of the family, and no one was really sure what he would do if ever confronted with Milton on a dark, lonely night.

Bundy Mac seemed okay. That is, the only run-ins they'd had had been cordial, but there was something in his eyes that gave Milton the shivers. It was the same with all the snakes that lived around here, though, even the black ones, whom Milton was certain he could beat up, if necessary. There were other snakes, though. Milton had only heard tales of them. Vipers, they called them: rattlesnakes and moccasins. They were something that gave Milton bad dreams. Yes, it was a dangerous world out here. But Milton would not be afraid.

That would require something akin to brains.

"Oh, I'm just going for a stroll," Milton replied to Oke's question. "It's a nice, moonlit night, and I thought I'd just go for a little walk."

"Someone left the door open?" Oke asked.

"Looks like it. Neat, huh?"

"I don't know about that," Oke said, looking to Star, who eyed Milton warily. "You know that owl, she's always around. You shouldn't be out here in the open. What's wrong with you?"

"What do you mean, what's wrong with me?" Milton glanced skyward. "I knew about that, the, uh, owl. Yeah, I knew that. So, I was just going out to the chicken coop, see what was going on over there. I'm staying near the fence. See? I think I know what I'm doing."

Milton looked around as if someone might be listening in, then asked, "Did you two know that barn owls are of the Ridgway family of owls?" Milton waited for a response, then said, "I didn't think so."

Oke and Star looked at each other.

"Well, don't let us stop you," Oke said. "You obviously know more about owls than we do."

Milton didn't like to throw his weight around, but he figured if you had it, you might as well flaunt it. That's what Pappy said. And what else could he do? Milton, living in Annie's room, was one of the most educated of ferrets possibly in the whole, entire world. At least, he was the smartest one around here.

Milton got to the end of the fence with Oke and Star right behind.

It seemed suddenly a long way across open ground to the chicken coop. The moon was up, and it was bright outside, so he would most assuredly see the owl coming. Right?

Milton had a sudden urge to maybe just head back home and crawl behind his nice, warm water heater with all his stuff – but he resisted it. The chicken coop. It was the Grail. The ultimate prize. He could get drunk on eggs, wallow in them, and maybe chase the chickens around the coop a couple times. Oh, it was tempting. He might never have a chance like this again.

He looked up at Oke and Star, their giant heads blocking out the moon and most of the sky. Then he looked back at the coop and up to the surrounding trees for any sign of that big barn owl – or even the great horned owl from off in the dark forest.

Now there was a scary-looking bird.

It seemed a long way, but Milton couldn't turn back now. Everyone would know. Oke was the biggest blabbermouth in the neighborhood.

He took one last look to the trees, especially the tall oaks out in the pasture. He took a deep breath and made his dash. The grass was thick here. He wished Uncle Amos would mow more often.

Then he saw it out of the corner of his eye, off in the distance: a dark shape emerging from the tall trees in the pasture, its fiendish wings outstretched like a demon from Hades. It seemed far away, but it was like in a dream when you can't move, you can't get your feet to move, as if they are filled with lead. The owl was getting bigger and bigger as Milton ran as fast as he could, which wasn't nearly as fast as he thought it was. That was something of which he was just now becoming aware, that he was pretty much fast only in the kitchen, with all the women.

They always said he was fast. But this owl, Milton noticed, seemed a lot faster.

With desperation, he ran. The shadow grew ever larger so that it blotted out the moon. He was almost there, only another few feet, but he had to get over the gutter drain pipe leading to the pig sty. He got a running leap and fell backwards. He looked up, and terror filled his heart. Turning back to the pipe, he gathered all his strength, will, and determination, and threw his all, almost two pounds, into it.

Oof!

He made it to the top, but he was in danger of sliding backwards. He clung to it desperately, his back legs clawing crazily. He struggled valiantly, his eyes looking to the swooping menace, the talons outstretched and grappling towards him at a dire, mighty speed.

"I ... almost ... got it," he gasped. Then he was over!

He looked up, and he knew it was too late. Yes, the wings of death blackened the sky. But he would not give up, even though it was hopeless. With bold determination, he made his final dash, except just as the great talons were about to envelope him, something else did; and he was all of a sudden out of the reach of the owl, in a dark, tight, enclosed space.

Something cold and wriggly pressed up against his body, as if it was all around him. It was cold, creepy, and slithery.

"AAAAAH!!!" Milton shrieked.

It was Bundy Mac! He had him in his coils! And he was going to swallow him whole!

What would be worse, Milton wondered, to be swallowed head or tail first? But there was no worry.

"You all right?" Bundy Mac said. "She almost got you, you know."

"You," Milton stammered. "You saved my life."

"No problem," Bundy Mac said. "The girl, she likes you. So I like you too. She saved me once from an anole that was about to beat me up when I was just a squirt."

"An anole? You must have been real little then, because they're real little."

"Yep," Bundy Mac said, "but I wasn't too young to appreciate her kindness. I promised then to make sure that there were never any rats around their house. That's why I have to come out here to find something to eat nowadays."

"Well, we all appreciate it, Mr. Mac."

"You can call me Bundy."

"Well, we all appreciate it, Bundy. I just heard Grandma saying the other day that she hasn't seen a rat or mouse in her house in years now."

Milton didn't mention that she had also given Kitty all the credit for it.

"So," Bundy Mac said. "What are you doin' out here?"

Milton nodded knowingly.

He pointed over his shoulder, and said, "Chicken coop."

"Oh, yes," Bundy Mac said, licking his lips with his forked tongue. "I was hopin' you were gonna say that. You'aaa, you got like, little people hands, don't you?"

Milton and Bundy Mac looked at his hands.

"They're small," Milton said, "but I've got a good grip."

"Wait right here," Bundy Mac said. "Let me pop my head out and see if that owl's still around. I got a plan."

"Oo, a plan," Milton said. "I love plans."

"Looks good," Bundy Mac said, drawing his head back in. Milton waited for him to go first, but Bundy Mac said, "You first, kid. It takes me a while to unravel."

Milton got a bad feeling. But he asked himself, what's an adventure without a little trepidation? Yes, an adventure! He felt like Mowgli in the Jungle Book. It was one of his favorite stories. He suddenly thought of Kaa, the giant python, and he looked at Bundy Mac, who wore a curious, Kaa-like smile on his sleek, shiny face. His forked tongue flicked hungrily, Milton thought.

No one would suspect Bundy of it if he did it. That is, there wouldn't be any evidence for them to pin the crime on him.

Milton felt silly and a little bad for thinking such a thing of Bundy Mac. He had saved his life!

He gulped. "Thank you, Kaa … I mean, Bundy."

Cautiously, he peeked out, all around and above and right over him, at the edge of the barn roof.

"Coast is clear," he said, and he crept out from the hole under the drainpipe. He took a deep breath and kept his eye out. No sign of the owl.

"I don't see him," Milton said.

"Oh, he's out there somewhere, watchin' us," Bundy Mac said as he slithered his impressive ten feet of length out of the cramped hole. He took the opportunity for a good stretch, then said, "Follow me. With those little hands of yours, I know a place we might be able to get in."

The plan was simple, like Uncle Amos.

Unlike Uncle Amos, the plan might work.

They passed along the front of the chicken coop, the hens expressing their displeasure with low, jittery clucking.

"Where's Cock-a-doodle-done-did at?"

Bundy Mac shrugged. "I don't know. He sleeps a lot. Probably up in the loft. He doesn't care anyway, as long as he gets what he wants, and he gets plenty of that."

Bundy Mac led him around the corner. He pointed at a space running behind the chicken coop. A minute later, they were looking into the coop through a broken slat.

"Ya see that? That slat is givin' me problems. If it were moved left an inch or two, I'd be able to get in there myself. But I can't move it. You see? It's kind of loose, but we need someone who can pull on it and move it left at the same time. See that?"

Milton's chest swelled.

It didn't happen often that someone asked for his help. It had never happened, in fact.

Milton had always wondered what it was like to be useful instead of just incredibly adorable.

"I sure do," he replied. "Why all I gotta do is get a good grip on it like this, and brace my feet like this, and give it a good ... Oooof! ... A good ... Umph! A good ... Ughh!" The chickens started moving around and making a fuss "How's that?" he said, breathing hard and looking with pride at his handiwork. "That's about as far as it will go."

"Outstanding!" Bundy Mac said, testing the hole for size. "It's a little tight," he said, squeezing himself through, the smooth scales on his sides crinkling and slithering past Milton, sending a shiver down his spine. "But good enough!" he declared with satisfaction. He coiled up comfortably and gave the shuddering, huddled hens at the end of the coop a once over.

Milton stared through the hole, into this wonderland of wonderlands. He easily squeezed through.

The chickens were all backed against the far wall, all their nests unoccupied and brimming with big, jumbo, smooth, scrumptious-looking eggs.

"All right, ladies," Bundy Mac said. "You all just stay right where you are, and there'll be no trouble, understand?"

They all clucked nervously. One of them, Matilda – definitely a roaster – was giving them the stink eye, but she remained as the rest, quiet and subdued.

Milton could hear them wondering among themselves where Cock-a-doodle-done-did might be.

Milton had never been so excited. He couldn't believe he was here, in the coop, his long-held dream, and he owed it all to Bundy Mac. He looked at him, muscling an egg down his throat. It was amazing, and it made Milton gag.

Milton didn't waste any time himself, selecting a nice, big juicy one; and he dove right in.

It truly was fun, hanging out with Bundy Mac, devouring eggs. His face, hands, arms, and everything else were encrusted in it. They kept on until Milton had to sit back and rest, his belly full, his life good. He looked over at Bundy Mac, who had the same expression on his sleek, snaky face: contentment.

They stayed like that a while, basking in their glory, when Bundy Mac turned his ear and said, "What's that? Did you hear that?"

Milton listened. Yes. There was something. It sounded like ... like –

"Darn it," Bundy Mac grumbled. He lifted his head and looked out towards the orange grove.

"What? What is it?"

"It's those darned raccoons."

"Raccoons?" Milton said. He had seen them before, at night sometimes, coming around the house, trying to get into Pappy's garbage cans. Pappy kept the cans chained down just because of raccoons. Pappy did not like raccoons. Grandma said they were cute, and Pappy said no they weren't: "A pestilence cannot be cute!"

"They're a nuisance," Milton commented. "That's what Pappy says."

"Well, he's right. They do nothin' but cause trouble. I wouldn't mind 'em so much," Bundy Mac sighed, "if they were smaller and I could get one of 'em down my gullet."

Milton gulped.

"So, what do we do now?"

"Nothin'. They can't get in here. They come most every night on their little, self-gratifying rampage, making their rounds and causing grief for everyone." He shook his head. "Always demanding everyone pay attention to them."

Milton got up on his legs and peered out the chicken wire at the gang of robbers approaching under the moonlight. He could hear them. They sounded like Cousin Kevin, from Brooklyn.

"Shut up, Pauly. Ya don't know what you're talkin' about."

"Oh, yeah?"

"Yeah."

"Oh, yeah?!"

"Yeah!"

And the two raccoons tore into each other.

The others shook their heads and kept on, directly for the coop.

"Hey!" the biggest raccoon finally said. "You two dumb-dolts cut it out! You're gonna wake up dat big dog up at da house!"

Milton's heart soared. They were talking about Buddy. His friend, Buddy, was the big dog.

"Look, kid," Bundy Mac said, yawning. "I don't really want to talk to these guys, so I'm heading out for a nap." He yawned again, exposing his wide, snaky mouth. A shiver ran down Milton's spine.

"Oh," he said. He had heard about snakes, how they could sleep for days after a meal. "Well, I guess I'll see you around then."

"Uh ... sure," Bundy Mac yawned. "Sure, kid. See you around."

Milton watched as he squeezed and slithered through the hole, the lumps along his length cracking one at a time, until the tip of his yellow and black, striped tail disappeared from view.

Milton turned, and there they were, all gathered around, peering in through the chicken wire at him. They stared.

Then one said, "What da heck is dat? Is dat a raccoon, Pauly?"

"Sure looks like one, Jacko," Pauly said. "Don't it, Sonny? Some kind 'a stunted raccoon or … somet'in'."

"Shut up, mo-rons," Sonny said, also in a New York accent. Then he turned to Milton, and asked, "What da heck are you anyways? You a raccoon?"

Milton wasn't sure what to say. He could see the slight resemblance, at least in the masked face and the pointy nose and beady eyes – and he couldn't help but notice the hands, which were very much like his.

He looked at them, and he found himself saying, "Yes. I'm a raccoon. My mother said I'm small-boned."

The other raccoons started laughing, but Sonny said, "All right, all right, all right." He looked at Milton with a wary eye. "How'd ya get in dea anyways?"

Milton pointed at the broken slat in the back.

Sonny looked at the hole, then Milton, and said, "Can ya bring eggs out'a dat hole?"

"Sure," Milton said, his chest puffing out. "You want me to bring you some?"

The raccoons all stared at him. They all started drooling and nodding.

"Yeah," Sonny said. "Dat's right. Yeah, we do."

"No problem," Milton said. "I'll meet you down at the other end. There's a gap there. It might take me a while. I'm kind of small, and these are jumbo-sized eggs, you know." The drooling intensified, and Milton added, "Big, jumbo-sized, juicy ones."

Chapter Six

Buddy didn't have to hear them. He could smell it, the scent of trouble.

Low down, lily-livered raccoons.

His first impulse was to look to Pappy, but Pappy couldn't see without his glasses and tended to just get up in the middle of the night and point his shotgun out the window in the general direction of the coop and shoot. He had shot more than a few chickens over the years that way – and yes, a couple of raccoons.

Buddy didn't have to be told not to like raccoons. It came as naturally as the revulsion to rats and cockroaches. The only difference was that Grandma thought they, raccoons, were cute.

Oh, yes. They were out there right now, wreaking havoc of some kind.

It was Buddy's job to protect the property from such criminal activity.

He got up and walked over to Grandma's side of the bed and stared at her lovely, sleeping face. He whined, gently. He set his giant, oversized head on the bed, and he stared. And he stared. And –

"Oh!" Big sigh. "What is it, Buddy?"

"Mmmmmm!"

"Can't you wait?"

"Mmmmmm!"

She looked at a conked out Pappy, then got up to take Buddy out. All the way down the stairs, she told him that he'd better not run off. Out the kitchen door Buddy went, leaving Grandma standing inside the screen.

Hey! Look! The utility room door is open! The rat got out! Look. LOOK!

Buddy stared at her, his eyes pleading, but she only said, "Well? Are you gonna go or not?"

Buddy sighed and nonchalantly ambled off to do his business, losing himself in the shadows of an oak tree and sniffing madly at the ground.

He could hear her, whispering loudly out the kitchen door, "Buddy! Don't you run off!"

But what else could he do, if she wasn't going to listen to him?

She'd thank him in the morning.

*   *   *

Milton had never worked so hard, but he had done it. He had cleared every last egg out of the coop with only one broken. He tried not to imagine Grandma's face when she came out to gather eggs and there would be none, but it was in the interest of adventure, exploration, and science! Who knew when he'd get a break like this again?

He sat down to rest against the drain pipe as the raccoons gathered up the spoils.

"You're all right, kid," Sonny said. "Even if ya are a short-staffed, skinny squoit, you're allll right in my book. Ain't dat right, boys?"

The boys, all covered in egg crusties, grinned and congratulated Milton, patting him on the back and shaking his hand.

"So, what's your name anyways?"

"Milton."

"Milton, huh? I suppose dat's all right. Ya hear dat, boys? Da squoit's name is Milton. And Milton, d'ese hea's da boys, and I'm Sonny Butz, da lead'a of dis gang."

"It's a real pleasure to meet you fellas," Milton said.

Sonny waved his hand, and said, "Get out'a hea."

Milton was enraptured. He was the man of the hour. Maybe of the whole day.

His stomach was troubling him, though. He might have eaten too much. But he could not be happier or more content.

"So," he said, "what's next?"

"Well," Sonny replied. "We gotta haul da loot back ta da Lodge, but on da way we might knock over a couple 'a gaa-bage cans."

"Yeah," Pauly said, "and did ya see dem toikeys roostin' in dem cypress trees back d'ere? Let's shake 'em up again! Dey're funny when dey first wake up."

"Dey are funny," Sonny said. "Toikeys," he shook his head. "I don't know who'd want'a be a toikey. I mean, da name itself. Come on. It's ridic-ilous."

"I don't know why anyone would want ta be anyt'ing but a raccoon," Jacko said.

The others all agreed.

They all looked at Milton, who swallowed hard, and stammered, "Oh. Uh, yes. I don't know why anyone would want to be anything but a raccoon."

The boys slapped him on the back, knocking him rolling, but Milton could only grin.

You're all right, kid!

"Sheesh!" Pauly said. "Dem's some mighty sharp lookin' teet' ya got d'ere."

The others gathered around to inspect Milton's tiny, pointy teeth.

"Would ya look at dat," Sonny said, and Milton swelled with pride.

At that very moment, they heard something.

The door to the house!

Light spilled from the door, and a yellow dusk stretched across the turnout to the coop.

The raccoons all looked at each other.

"Prob'ly dat doity dog!" Sonny warned. "Come on, boys! Let's get out'a hea!"

As they grabbed up their plunder, Milton stood there, transfixed on the light from the door.

Sonny grabbed him by the collar. He slapped him twice across the face.

"What'a ya doin'?!" he said. "We gotta make our getaway!"

"Huh? Getaway?"

"Yeah! Da getaway!" Sonny said, grasping Milton by the collar. "On my back!" And before Milton could respond, Sonny had tossed him onto his back; and they dashed away, across the barnyard and the grassy lane, under the split-rail fence, and into the darkness of the orange grove.

*   *   *

Buddy felt bad about Grandma.

She would wait a while, then go up and wake Pappy. He would come down and call for him, then he would sit in the kitchen chair, eating cereal or sleeping with his head on the table next to his empty cereal bowl until he woke up. Then he would stick his head out the door and call for him, Buddy, and go back to the living room and sleep in his easy chair until he heard a scratching at the door.

Then he'd open it, and say, "Bad Dog!"

Then they'd go upstairs and go back to bed.

By the time Buddy got to the coop, the robbers had high-tailed it. He dashed here and there, sniffing madly – licking at some of the egg drippings, just for evidence's sake – then he stopped at the turnout.

"You guys see anything?"

"Sure," Oke said. "Milton got mixed up with those bad boys, now he's run off with them. Lord have mercy," he said with a big, donkey sigh, "I knew all this would turn out bad, but I didn't know it would turn out this bad. Our own little Milton, joined up with a gang of bad men – or raccoons, same thing."

"You sure," Buddy said skeptically, glancing at Star.

The big horse shrugged, and said, "I wasn't really paying attention, but it did look like he was in on it. Shoot, if you ask me, he was the instigator."

They all gazed upon the scene of the crime. There was egg yolk everywhere, like some kind of egg soirée.

"Darn it," Buddy mumbled.

"Yep," Oke agreed. "Darn it."

"All right," Buddy said. "I guess I gotta go after him."

"Yep," Oke replied. "I guess you do."

Star nodded.

Buddy put his nose to the ground, and said, "It won't be hard findin' 'em, though. They smell like eggs – and raccoons."

He started on his way, towards the orange grove, but Oke said, "All right, all right, all right. I'll help."

Buddy stopped, turned, and said, "You?"

"Of course, me," Oke snapped. "You don't think King Kong here can negotiate that orange grove, do you?"

He looked askance at Star, who gave Oke the you-do-whatever-you-want look.

"It's true," Oke said. "You're mighty big and tough, Buddy, but you can't take on a whole gang of raccoons all by yourself. That's suicide. True, they might be nothing more than hooligans, but they can be pretty rough characters, I assure you."

"But, how you gonna get out of the pen?" Buddy queried.

Oke rolled his eyes. "Don't you worry about me, dog." And he hurried off, around the corner of the barn.

Buddy and Star looked at each other. They didn't really have a lot in common except for the daily chase down the fence line.

"So ... been hot."

"Mm-hm."

"For this time of year."

"Yep."

Star just wasn't much of a talker, but it wasn't necessary because Oke appeared around the other corner of the barn.

"How did you do that?" Buddy asked.

"I always keep one escape route at the ready, just in case of a situation like this."

Buddy nodded his approval.

"It's nothin'," Oke mumbled. Then he said, "Lead the way, oh leader. Forward we march, hot on the trail of those scurrilous, masked devils."

Chapter Seven

"Hey look, fellas!" Jacko said. "It's a gopher toitoise!"

"Oh, boy!" everyone exclaimed.

They set their loads down and watched with fascination as Jacko went over to a slowly escaping tortoise, picked him up, and turned him around.

The boys all laughed and waited while the tortoise slowly stuck his arms and legs and head back out, then proceeded on, making a wide arc to get back to his original course.

Jacko grinned and did it again, and they all laughed.

Milton laughed too, though he didn't really see that it was so funny the second time, or the third time, or even less the fourth. Then Pauly turned the tortoise on his back, and everyone laughed harder than ever. Milton didn't really get it. He kind of just stared, but then the others started looking at him, so he laughed along.

The raccoons had their fun, then Sonny said, "All right, boys. Let's get out'a hea. Gotta get ta da Lodge wid dis mud'a-lovin' haul."

"But," Milton said as they were leaving, down the pine forest trail, "aren't you gonna set him back on his feet?"

Sonny only waved his hand, and said, "Get out'a hea."

Milton stared after them a moment. He couldn't just leave the tortoise like that, so he hurried back to help him, which wasn't easy. He was a big one, this Larry. Milton had seen him around.

At one point, Larry almost rolled over on top of Milton, trapping him underneath. Finally, thanks to Milton's little human-like hands, he was able to utilize a big stick to leverage him enough so that Larry could claw his way over and onto his feet.

"Whew! Thanks," Larry said. "I don't know what I'd have done."

"It's no problem, Larry," Milton said. "But I better get going and catch up with my friends."

"Those are your friends?" Larry asked.

"Uh … well, yeah. Sure. We were just going back to their Lodge."

The tortoise looked him over, and said, "You look different from them. Not just smaller, but different."

"Oh, that's because I'm really a ferret."

"A ferret? What's that?"

"It's what I am," Milton said. "I live up at the house."

"Oh. The house," Larry repeated. "Well," he said, "if you want to catch up with them, you'd better hurry."

Milton looked up the trail, at the sparkles of moonlight glittering the forest floor, then back at Larry.

* * *

Okey Donkey was a natural leader of men – or whatever.

Not only that, he struck fear in the heart of all raccoons; as would any donkey.

Donkeys don't put up with that kind of behavior – gallivanting around at night, breaking and entering and looting.

He often wondered what it was about raccoons that made them so unruly and without manners. They never greeted anyone – no "Good morning!" or "Good afternoon!" But then, in the end, it was usually better when they didn't say anything at all.

It never stopped, every time they came around.

Of the many dimwitted, unhumorous "ass" remarks Oke endured, most of the lowest caliber material came from the raccoons.

They were just rude, and crude, and sometimes lewd. In fact, very often lewd.

He wasn't afraid of them, though. Yes, he understood they were tough guys, that it wasn't all talk and bluster. There were plenty of stories. Just a few weeks ago, a big one got ahold of Mrs. Dobson's dog and gave him a pretty good pummeling, according to Oke's sources.

But Oke wasn't a dog.

If he'd had the opportunity, he could have killed that coyote he was credited with killing, if he could have caught him – and if he wasn't so fat. But that was beside the point. Everyone knows that nobody messes with the donkey, unless they want to get their cabbage kicked in.

Oke never had a doubt. As soon as Buddy showed up, he knew he'd be going along. Donkeys dream of adventure and even conquest. Most people are not aware of it, but it was not Sancho Panza that led Don Quixote on his quest, as is generally believed. It was Sancho Panza's donkey, Ed, that led the way.

It was part of Oke. It simmered in his hot, Spanish blood: the insatiable lure of adventure and conquest.

Oke wasn't sure about the Spanish part, but that's the way he liked to think about it.

He looked over his shoulder to Star and gave him a wink. He knew his buddy would be worried about him.

The first obstacle was the split-rail fence that separated the orange grove from the rest of the farm. Buddy had to wait for Oke while he went down to the opening by the creek and hurried back.

"Is that as fast as you can run?" Buddy asked.

"Not at all," Oke replied. "I have several speeds, and that one was adequate for these purposes. Now, shall we proceed?"

Traversing the orange grove was not a problem, but that ended at the pine forest, where the going got trickier. There were fallen trees, branches, and saw palmetto, as well as vines in some places that were difficult to get around.

Oke was impressed with Buddy's olfactory senses, the way he just put his nose to the ground and barreled ahead, under, over, and around everything. For Oke, however, it was getting ever more difficult to keep up. He had quit trying to follow Buddy exactly, and just started stomping his way through the forest behind him. Even that was difficult, though, with all of Buddy's jumping over trees and branches, and worse, crawling under them.

"What do you mean, you can't crawl?"

"I can't crawl. My legs don't do like yours do."

Donkey and dog looked at donkey's legs, comparing them to dog's legs.

"Well, go ahead and try," Buddy said.

Oke sighed. He got down on his knees, and he tried. And he tried – *Ouch! Ow! Ouch! Ow! Ow!* And Buddy laughed so hard that he rolled over onto his back, holding his stomach it hurt so much.

So now, Buddy had to wait at all major obstacles so Oke could go around.

Buddy suddenly stopped.

"Wait a minute," he said.

"What is it?" Oke asked.

Buddy sniffed up the trail, then back down. A scowl creased his heavy, brown brow.

"All I can smell is eggs."

"Well, just follow that smell."

Buddy looked at him, like, *I know that.*

Oke rolled his shoulders. "Hey, I'm just tryin' to help here."

"Someone else has been here recently," Buddy said, deep in thought. "It smells like gopher."

"Tortoise?'

"Yeah."

"So?'

"So, it's just throwing me off is all. You don't know what it's like to get your sniffer all in a tizzy. First it's eggs, now it's gopher, not to mention it's the whole gol-diggin' forest! I got about a thousand different scents to deal with here … and … what do I look like, a bloodhound?!"

"Whoa! Sorry, my man. You're the tracker here. We're followin' you. You lead the way."

"I'm sorry," Buddy sighed. "I shouldn't have snapped at you like that, but this could be serious, you know. He's a total idiot."

"He is that," Oke replied. "He just doesn't understand the dangers of the world. It's like he's –"

"Stupid."

"Yeah. Stupid. Anyway, he's a good little guy, and Annie would be sad if something happened to him."

"Yeah," Buddy sighed. "Annie would be sad. So," he said, studying the trail, "something happened here with a gopher. The egg-ferret-raccoon smell splits off here, along with the scent of tortoise."

Oke pondered.

Then he said, "I think we should follow the main trail. Don't you?"

"I think so," Buddy replied, and they continued on, ever deeper into the Big Hammock.

*   *   *

Milton was lost.

He was back in the pine forest, wandering aimlessly, but enjoying every minute of it.

Freedom, he had discovered, was not overrated.

Pappy said freedom, personal freedom to say and think and do whatever you want, was the most precious commodity on earth. He said it was one of the only things worth dying for, individual liberty for all men – and ferrets. Milton had thrown the last part in himself.

It was magnificent, the pine forest in the moonlight. He liked the way the pine needles lay flat under his feet, like Grandma's living room rug. And he couldn't get over the tall, straight trees all around him, reaching to the sky. They looked mysterious in the blanched moonlight that filtered through the distant tops. He walked with wonder emanating from his beady eyes. He passed a rabbit, out foraging. They said their hellos, and Milton would have continued the conversation, but the rabbit didn't seem interested.

He met a frog, and asked him the way to the Lodge, but he didn't know.

The many aromas of this strange, new world wafted up from the soil, and they enveloped him from above, all of them wondrous and enticing. To Milton, the amalgamation smelled just like freedom.

"Ah, that smells good!"

"Why, thank you."

Milton caught his breath. He turned to find himself face to face with a skunk. And not just a skunk, but a skunk in a cage!

He had never seen one, a skunk, but he knew what they were from Annie's many books on nature and science. He had heard tales, and he wasn't sure whether to be excited or nervous or just run away.

"Oh! Hello," he said, backing away just a tad.

The skunk sighed. "I only squirt if I'm in danger. Am I in danger?"

"Oh! Not from me," Milton said. "My name's Milton. I'm a ferret … from up at the house."

"The house, huh? What are you doing out here, then? My name's Patty, by the way."

"Nice to meet you, Patty."

"So," Patty said. "I noticed you have opposable thumbs. You think you could'aaa help me out here? I wouldn't have fallen for the old bait in the trap trick, except the bait was bacon and peanut butter. Darn it."

"Mm, I do like bacon and peanut butter," Milton said as he tried to figure out the hasp on the door.

"It's old man Perkins' trap. I've beaten it a few times, you know. He has them scattered around the forest here. I don't know what I was thinking."

"You were thinking bacon and peanut butter."

"Yes, I was," Patty chuckled. "So, what are you doing out here in the forest?"

"Oh," Milton said with pride, "I'm on an adventure. I mean, I wouldn't be, but I escaped. I mean someone, Pappy most likely, left the door open to the utility room, so now I'm taking a vacation here in the forest. Anyway, I was hanging out with the raccoons over at the coop, and –"

"Raccoons?"

"Yeah, and I was –"

"You were hanging out with the raccoons? Why were you hanging out with them?"

"Well, I guess because they were nice to me."

"Nice to you? Why were they nice to you? They're raccoons. They don't like anyone but raccoons."

"Oh, well, they think I'm a raccoon." Milton's chest swelled. "I got them a whole load of eggs from the coop."

"Oh?" Patty said, taking interest.

"I sure did."

"Well," she said, "their Lodge is somewhere in the Big Hammock, down that trail, but I wouldn't advise you go there. You can come with me if you want, though."

"Where are you going?"

"I don't know. Any of those eggs left?"

"Not a one," Milton stated proudly.

Once again, Milton had to decide: which way to go? He really wanted to see that Lodge, after all the talk about it. The raccoons had said it was palatial – and lots of fun. They said they had alcohol there. And women.

He wondered if there would be cookies.

*   *   *

Buddy was beginning to regret bringing Oke along. Sure, he was tough and smart, but his legs didn't even work the right way! It was one of the most ridiculous things he'd ever seen.

"What are you laughing at up there?" Oke said.

"Oh, nothing. Just a joke I heard the other day."

Buddy knew Oke was sensitive about such things, his inadequacies.

Pappy said everyone had them, inadequacies; everyone except for Buddy. Pappy said Buddy was the only one of God's creatures he had ever seen that had no inadequacies, not even a little one. The perfect porch dog, he called him. That's what he said, the perfect dog! At least that's what he'd say after a few beers.

At the moment, Buddy didn't want to know what Pappy thought of him.

He had to concentrate on his mission.

They stopped to talk to a roosting woodpecker, who had given them further directions.

"What are you g-g-g-g-goin' there for?" he had asked.

Buddy, who was waiting for Oke to catch up, replied, "We think they've kidnapped one of our friends, or something like that."

"Really? Who did they kidnap-p-p-p-p?"

"Milton the ferret."

"Ferret-t-t-t? What's a ferret-t-t-t-t?"

Buddy shrugged. "He looks kind of like a really, really scrawny otter, but with a pointier nose and beadier eyes, and he doesn't seem afraid of anything. Oh, and he has a mask."

"A mask-k-k-k-k?"

"Yeah, you know. Kind of like the raccoons do."

"A rob-b-b-b-b-ber's mask?"

49

"Right. I mean kind of. He's not a robber, except for, well, tonight he helped the raccoons to take the eggs in the coop. But me and Oke think it was under duress."

"D-d-d-d-duress?"

Buddy shrugged. It wasn't really the woodpecker's business.

"Well, good luck-k-k-k-k, 'cause you're gonna need it. No one's ever been in the Raccoon Lodge before … not anyone that made it b-b-b-b-back out, that is."

Buddy gulped. Everyone said the same thing.

He looked, and there was Oke, stomping his way through the forest.

"Whew! Hey, fellas." Oke looked up in the tree, then at Buddy. "Aren't you gonna introduce me to your friend?"

"Oh, yeah," Buddy said. "Uh, Woody, this is Oke. He's the donkey I was telling you about."

"I'm Woodson MacGregor," the woodpecker said. Woody looked at Oke critically, then said, "You mean the one that k-k-k-k-killed the coyote?"

Buddy nodded, and he glanced at Oke, who shrugged modestly.

"You're shorter than I thought you'd b-b-b-b-be."

"That's right," Oke replied. "We call it compact and efficient."

"And," Woodson added. "You're a lot … … fat-t-t-t-ter than I thought you'd be too."

Buddy suppressed a chuckle as Oke stood a little straighter, and said with a note of defiance, "That's the efficient part. I can go without eating for a very long time and simply live off the fat I've stored up, especially along the back of my neck."

"I was gonna ask what that giant growth was on the back of your neck-k-k-k-k."

Oke scowled.

"It's not a growth. It's my mane. It's like a camel's hump, all right? It has a purpose. All right?"

"All right, all right," Woodson replied. "I was just wondering."

"Hmph," Oke grumbled.

"It's true," Buddy said in support of his friend. "Grandma says he is compact and efficient. And Pappy says he's a badass."

They said their goodbyes, and once again were off, leaving behind the pine forest and proceeding onward, into the Big Hammock. The jungle was dark and foreboding – and way, way harder to negotiate for one who cannot climb over or crawl under.

Chapter Eight

Buddy and Oke continued on, through the forest. They came around a bend in the trail, and coming right towards them was a possum who, upon spotting Buddy, froze in his tracks and keeled over onto his side. He lay there, unmoving, his eyes glassy, his teeth bared.

Buddy and Oke looked at each other and sighed.

Then Buddy said, "I don't have time now, Elwood. Me and Oke here are busy."

Buddy sighed, and looked to Oke. Then he shook the lifeless-looking possum.

"Hey. Elwood. Wake up. I don't have time now. Hey. Elwood. Do you know where the Raccoon Lodge is? Hey. Snap out of it."

Elwood didn't move a muscle.

"Fine," Buddy said, and they continued on.

*   *   *

Milton followed Patty's directions, and he was making good time. He couldn't be sure, of course. Actually, he didn't know where he was. The terrain had changed from pine to hammock. The jungle floor here was different, not as clean. It was damp. It smelled different, mustier – menacing. Something strange stirred inside Milton, something unfamiliar.

Worry, uneasiness, and disquietude are things foreign to a ferret.

"Sssssssssssss."

Milton's skin crawled, and he looked to see a cottonmouth moccasin, leering at him from under some ferns. He froze.

The snake's thick, coarse body was coiled. He lay, murderously, within striking distance. His tail quivered, and his forked tongue flicked sinisterly: in and out; in and out.

"Sssssssssssss."

His wicked, muck-colored head moved slowly back and forth. His black, wicked eyes seemed to penetrate deep, deep into Milton's.

"Sssssssssssss."

"I don't know what you are," he hissed, "but you look delicioussssssssssss."

"Oh," Milton stammered, frozen in place by the serpent's wicked gaze. "I'm not. You can ask Kitty. She'll tell you. I mean, she doesn't really know, but she says rats don't taste that good, and I probably don't either."

"Oh," the moccasin replied. "Rats are delicioussssssssssss. And I think you are too."

It all came crashing down on Milton.

This is what they all meant when they said it was dangerous out here. I can't run to Annie now. I can't even run to Pappy. I'm on my own. So this is it. This is how it all ends. In the belly of a lowly moccasin.

Oh, the travesty!

Milton had heard one was not supposed to move with a moccasin, but he thought that was just for humans and other animals too big for moccasins to actually swallow whole. Not ferrets!

He made a plan. Without moving his head, he looked to the left, then the right. He'd have to move fast and with deliberation. One movement, then run for it!

I mean, how fast can a moccasin be? 'Cause I'm pretty fast.

Milton remembered the owl and how slow he had felt.

But a snake? I can certainly outrun a snake, especially a big fat one like that.

Milton tried to look away from the cold, hypnotizing eyes. He couldn't.

Oh, no! It's true! I've been hypnotized! Oh, the horror!

Then there came a light from heaven, a voice from beyond. From New York, in fact:

"Dea ya are, ya little, short-staffed, skinny squoit! We wondered where ya went off to."

Milton remained frozen in place.

"Whoa! Lookee dea! Look at dat, boys. Our little pal's in trouble. Hey, snake," Sonny said.

"Yesssssssssss?" the snake hissed.

"Wha'd'ya t'ink you're doin'? Dat's a raccoon you're messin' wid. What's wrong whi'ch you?"

"That'sssssssssss no raccoon," the snake replied. "The bone structure is all wrong. He's too sssssssssssvelt, and sssssssssssssmooth." She flicked her tongue hungrily.

"Look, snake. Is it woith havin' da whole district all over your back? If it is, go ahead." He looked to the boys. "Ain't dat right, boys?"

Jacko and Pauly nodded. They bared their teeth.

"Sssssssssssss," Pauly said.

"Yeah," Jacko snickered. "Sssssssssssss."

The snake transfixed them with her eyes, and they quickly averted their gazes.

"Sssssssssss. Fine. Take your little underweight friend. Hardly any meat on those bones anyway."

With that, the snake slithered away, into the dark and dankness of the jungle floor.

"Gee," Milton said. "Thanks. You saved my life!"

Sonny waved his hand. "Get out'a hea," he said, and he ambled away, down the trail. "Dis time try ta keep up. We're almost d'ea."

Milton looked to Jacko and Pauly, who were arguing over whose turn it was to go last.

"I'll go last!" Milton volunteered.

They paused from their arguing to look at Milton.

"No," Jacko said. "If we lose ya again, Sonny'll kill us. We'll shoot for it."

"All right," Pauly said. "Best two out'a three."

"Right," Jacko replied.

Ten minutes later – after several rounds of rock, paper, scissors – they were up to best twenty-five out of forty-nine.

"How about I just do Eeny-meeny-miny-mo?" Milton suggested.

The boys looked at each other and nodded.

A minute later Pauly was "it."

"Wait a minute," he said. "Is 'it' last? Or is 'it' not last?"

Milton looked at them, glanced down the trail, and said, "It's uh ... last. 'It' goes last."

Pauly scowled, and mumbled, "Fine. Let's go," and the three of them headed up the trail for the famed and fabled Raccoon Lodge.

"You missed all the fun at the Smith's garbage can," Pauly said as they walked away.

"Really?"

"Yeah. Da kid forgot ta put da lid on it again. It was great!" Jacko said. "D'ea was a whole pot of leftover mac and cheese in d'ea."

"Darn it. I love leftover mac and cheese."

"Who doesn't?"

*   *   *

"I think that turkey back there gave us bad directions."

"I think so too."

"Keep your eyes open for someone to ask."

Buddy and Oke were skirting a cypress forest. In the distance, through the trees, they could make out the sheen of water. Rising from it were the gray-ash trunks of the aged behemoths. Moonlight filtered through the trees, making an apropos setting for a storybook fantasy. The mist, hanging just over the water's surface, suggested a tale of the mystical and foreboding.

"Who."

"Who what?"

"I didn't say anything."

"Who."

As one, they looked up, high up into the branches of a towering cypress tree, to see the great horned owl.

"Oh!" they said in unison. "Hello!"

"Who ... are you?"

Buddy glanced at Oke, and said, "We're from up at the house, up the end of the grassy lane. I'm Buddy, the dog, and this is Oke, the donkey."

"A long way from home," the owl said in a noble tone. "And what are you doing here, this late at night? The forest can be a dangerous place for house animals at night."

"Yes," Buddy agreed, glancing at Oke. "We know that. That's why we're here. One of our friends, well, he broke out of the utility room and into the chicken coop, and now he's run off with, well, we think he may have been –"

Buddy looked to Oke, who said, "He's a ferret."

"A ferret? What in the world is that?"

"It's like an elongated rat but with a furry tail and a better disposition."

The owl looked down at them with curiosity.

"A rat with a personality, you say?"

"Yes. That's it. And he's a little cuter than a rat too."

"That is true," Oke attested. "He is *much* cuter than a rat."

"So I hear," the owl said.

"You ... heard already?"

"News travels fast in the forest," the owl said. "And we have our own, shall we say, assistants? It is good to be king, you know."

"Oh. Oh! Yes," Buddy replied. "We've heard that before, about you." He elbowed Oke. "Right?"

"Huh? Oh! Yes!" Oke stated with certainty. "Many, many times!"

They looked at each other.

Buddy whispered, "Do we bow or curtsey?"

Oke thought a minute, then said, "Boys bow. Girls curtsey."

"Right," Buddy said.

They both made solemn attempts at bows that actually looked more like curtseys – and not very good ones.

They could see the king was pleased, however.

"So anyway, King … uh –"

"You may call me Ambrosius. King Ambrosius."

"So, King Ambrosius," Buddy continued, "what exactly do you know about our predicament?"

King Ambrosius shrugged. "Most everything, we suppose. Your idiotic little friend, who is not a raccoon, is at this minute on his way to the Raccoon Lodge, where he will be discovered for what he is, eventually. Then he will be killed, probably tortured first – possibly even sacrificed."

Buddy looked at Oke. Both swallowed hard.

Sacrificed?

"From what my royal sources tell me," King Ambrosius went on, "it is not a pleasant place for anyone to be who is not a raccoon."

Buddy and Oke looked at each other. Trepidation spilled from their eyes.

"You would do well to find him before he arrives there, but beware! The closer you come to the Lodge, the more dangerous it becomes for you. They have scouts and spies everywhere, just as we have ours. They may even be aware of your presence and are, at this moment, sending out reconnaissance parties." King Ambrosius looked way, way over his shoulder. He lowered his voice. "You must beware. And you must trust no one."

"But," Buddy queried, "we can trust you?"

There was an extended pause.

"Yes. But in general, it is always better not to trust too much."

Buddy did not like the sound of that. What was he saying? To trust him or not?

"Those are wise words," Buddy said, glancing at Oke. "So, can you give us directions? To the Lodge?"

"Yes. I can."

"And do you know where he is now?"

"Not at this moment, but from what I hear, he is presently traveling with two of the raccoons. They are on the South Trail leading in, while you are on the North Trail. In my judgement, which is sound – I am an owl, after all – I suggest you take the Loop Trail and cut him off before he gets there – if it's not too late already."

Buddy gulped. It wasn't what he wanted to hear.

King Ambrosius went on to give them explicit directions, then he said, "I must caution you. It is a fool's mission. From here on, you will be traveling through raccoon-held territory. You will be on your own. They may have already laid traps for you, so you must be aware of your surroundings at all times. At every turn, you must be clever, intuitive, and cunning."

Buddy gulped again. Pappy said he didn't have a clever, intuitive, cunning bone in his whole body. He hoped Oke did.

"We understand," Buddy replied. "We'll be ready."

King Ambrosius looked down on them, his wide, clear, insightful eyes taking them in. Then he sighed and shook his head with reverence and solemnity.

"You are brave and honorable souls, Buddy the dog and Okey the donkey, there is no doubt. But whether you be judged heroes or fools, that can only be determined by your ultimate success or failure. Your chances are small, but your courage and determination are great. It is in your hands – so to speak – what may become a good and righteous destiny. So, as I send you off, I bid you good luck, fare thee well, and Godspeed."

A few minutes later, the two rescuers proceeded ever further into the depths of the Big Hammock, deep, deep into raccoon-held territory.

"Darn it. I wanted to ask him if there was a 'regular' horned owl, in addition to the 'great' one?"

"Yeah. Me too."

*　　*　　*

ORRR-*ROAR*RRRRRR-ARRRRR-Owwww!!

"What's that?!" Milton gasped.

All three looked around nervously.

"I think it's a truck with a flat tire out on the highway."

ORRR-*ROAR*RRRRRR-ARRRRR-Owwww!!!

"No," Pauly mumbled. "It sounds more like a lion, or a bear. Whoever it is, they sound ticked off."

The boys looked nervously over their shoulders.

"Shouldn't we investigate?" Milton asked. "It sounds like someone might need help."

"Help?" Jacko said. He and Pauly snickered and carried on.

"Well," Milton said, "I think we should at least take a look. What if it was you that needed help?"

They both turned. Perplexed expressions.

Huh?

"I said, what if it was you that needed help? And no one came?"

"Now, just hold on a minute d'ea," Jacko said. "Dat sounds suspiciously like pinko talk. Ain't dat what it's called, Pauly? Pinko talk?"

"Yeah. Dat's right. Pinko talk. It's fun ta say, ain't it? Pinko talk?"

"Yeah. It's fun ta say," Jacko said. "Pinko talk."

They looked at Milton, who shrugged, and said, "If it was one of you, I'd come to help."

Once again, the boys seemed stumped.

ORRR-*ROAR*RRRRRR-ARRRRR-Owwww!!!

"Of course, you'd come ta help us," Pauly said. "We're raccoons. It's part 'a da Code: Raccoons help Raccoons. Everyone else can stick it."

"Uh, right," Milton said, coming to grips with what it meant to be a raccoon and why no one liked them. He sighed, in a defeatist way.

But then he took a deep breath, and said, "Well, you like me, don't you?"

"You kiddin' us?!" Jacko exclaimed. "You're tops, kid. Who'd'ya t'ink we owe all dis sweet loot to?" He nodded at his bag of plunder. Eggs: the gold standard.

"Dat's right, kid," Pauly agreed. "You're tops wid us!"

"And you'd help me if I needed help?"

ORRR-*ROAR*RRRRRR-ARRRRR-Owwww!!!

"Ya kiddin'? We'd be d'ea in a flash."

"Dat's right. Like greeeeased t'oity-eights!" Jacko said.

"Yeah," Pauly repeated. "Greeeeased t'oity-eights!"

They high-fived.

ORRR-*ROAR*RRRRRR-ARRRRR-Owwww!!!

"Well, I have news, fellas. And I hope you don't take it wrong, or decide you don't like me after all, but –"

"Decide not ta like ya?! Get out'a hea!"

"Well, I sure hope so," Milton said, taking another deep breath, "because I am not a raccoon. I'm a … a ferret."

Jacko and Pauly stared at him, mouths agape, as if he had just declared that eggs are bad for you.

Milton stared back, feeling a little nervous and wondering if telling them had been a bad idea.

Then Pauly slapped Jacko on the back, and said, "Why, dis one's a real kidd'a, ain't he, Jacko?! A ferret! Whoever hoid of a ferret?!"

Jacko's eyes lit up with relief, and he laughed just as hard.

"He's just a big kidd'a, ain't he?! You're a big kidd'a, ain't ya, kid? You're just pullin' our legs, ain't ya? Ya big kidd'a, you!"

Milton gave it some thought.

Then he shook his head, and said, "No, it's true. I'm a ferret, not a raccoon. I live up at the house with the little girl."

Jacko and Pauly looked him over. Their brows furrowed deeply. Then they looked to each other, and the hair stood up on the backs of their necks. Milton could see their lips curling and their teeth baring. Slowly, their eyes settled on him.

They crossed their arms and looked him over. They mumbled among themselves.

"I reckon I can see some differences now," Jacko said.

"Yeah," Pauly agreed. "Like, he's a lot smaller'n us, ain't he?"

"Yeah, and he's long and skinny, like one of dem smarmy, show-offy otters."

"Yeah, dem smarmy, show-offy otters."

"And get a load 'a dem ridic-ilous lookin' short legs."

"Yeah. Da only t'ing dat looks like a raccoon is his mask, and his tiny, raccoon-like fingers."

"Yeah."

"Yeah."

They stared at Milton, standing there looking back at them.

Jacko finally shook his head, and said, "He is cute, d'ough, ain't he?"

"Yeah. He's cute, all right. And he did get us all d'ese eggs. Wait till the boys back at da Lodge get a load 'a d'ese melons!"

"Yeah."

"Yeah."

They studied him some more.

Finally, Pauly said, "I gotta tell ya, d'ough. Da mask and da hands, dat's good enough for me."

"Me too," Jacko nodded. "All right, kid. So, what do we do now? Go get gobbled up by an angry be'ya?"

Milton shrugged, and said, "It's up to you. But I think we should at least go investigate. Don't you?"

The boys sighed and shook their heads. They set their things down and went to investigate the strange noise that sounded disquietingly like an angry bear. Jacko led the way because he was *not* "it."

Slowly, they crept through the forest, listening to a sporadic series of ORRR-*ROAR*RRRRRR-ARRRRR-Owwww!!!s.

They were hiding in the bushes.

"See? It's a be'ya."

"What's wrong with her?" Milton asked.

"She's stuck in da be'ya trap, dat's what."

"Better her d'an me," Pauly said.

"Yeah. Me too."

"You shouldn't say that," Milton said. "Grandma says even if you feel things like that, you shouldn't say them."

"Why not?"

"For many reasons," Milton said. "But mostly for common courtesy."

"Common coi'tesy?"

"Yes. But also, according to Pappy, because of Karma."

"Kaa'ma?"

"Yep. That's when good things happen to you because you did good things, and bad things happen because you did bad things. Pappy says it's basically the same thing as, 'You get what you deserve.'"

Jacko and Pauly looked at each other. They swallowed hard.

"You mean," Jacko said, "if I'm like some sissy boy, and I'm nice and pleasant ta ud'as, d'en good t'ings'll happen ta me?"

"Sort of, I suppose."

"Now, hold on a minute hea," Pauly said. "We been bad every day of our lives, and look how t'ings have toined out for us."

The boys looked at each other, then at Milton.

He shrugged, and said, "I was just saying –"

"Yeah, yeah, yeah," Pauly said. "So anyways, I ain't goin' near dat thing. Not only is it a be'ya; it's a TICKED OFF be'ya!"

"Just let me talk to her," Milton said. "She's staked to the ground, right? She can't chase me ... can she?"

The boys shrugged.

With that, Milton said, "Wish me luck," which the boys did.

He stepped out into the open. The bear saw him, and ORRR-*ROAR*RRRRRRR-ARRRRR-Owwww!!!

A gust of air brushed past Milton, and he realized the size and power of the bear.

"He-hello," he said, waving meekly.

The bear looked at him, and said, "What do you want?"

Milton dared to step closer.

"Well," he said, "my name's Milton, just so you know. And it looks like you got stuck in the trap."

The bear stared, obviously in pain, and said, "No kiddin', Sherlock." She looked down at the trap snapped firmly around her leg.

"That looks like it must hurt."

"Oh, really? You think so?"

The bear rolled her eyes and looked like she was about to let out a giant ORRR-*ROAR*RRRRRRR-ARRRRR-Owwww!!!

Milton said, "Maybe I can help."

Instead of a giant ORRR-*ROAR*RRRRRRR-ARRRRR-Owwww!!!, the bear started laughing: Hahahahahahaha-owowow.

Milton waited. He did understand the humor.

"I have help with me," he said, "if you want it ... but only if you promise not to beat us up or eat us."

"Us?"

"Right. Me and my two friends, in the bushes over there. Hey, fellas. Let … what's your name, ma'am?"

"Uh … Betty. Betty Bear."

The bushes across the way quivered. Then two heads appeared. Jacko and Pauly waved.

"Oh, great," Betty said. "Raccoons. Uh, no thanks. I don't need any help. I don't know what you three are up to, but I don't have any cash, no jewelry, no fresh garbage, so just go, and don't come back. And you too," she said to Milton, "whatever the heck you are – just go!"

"I'm a ferret."

"Yeah, well, whatever. I don't need any help from any raccoons or ferrets, whatever that is. What are you, some kind of cub scout raccoon? Learning the ropes of rude, obnoxious behavior? What do you guys have planned? Some way to torture me? Humiliate me? To ruin my last moments on earth before old Farmer Perkins shows up and shoots me full of holes and mounts my head over the fireplace and lays my skin on the floor in front of it?"

It was a lot for Milton to take in.

He thought about it, then he said, "Well, it looks to me like we're the only chance you got."

Betty Bear eyed Milton, then the boys, who watched quietly from the bushes.

Then she said, "Fine. What's your plan?"

"Well," Milton said. "I suppose we need to make one, but it looks to me like a simple spring-loaded mechanism with a locking device of some sort. I think between the three of us, we can get you free." He paused. "But you have to promise not to beat us up afterward. Or eat us."

"I promise," Betty said. "Why, if you guys can get me out of this fix, I'll be forever in your debt."

"Oo," Milton said, looking to the boys. "Forever in our debt, she says. That sounds like a good thing, doesn't it? Having a bear for a friend?"

Jacko looked at Pauly, and said, "Sounds okay ta me."

"Yeah. Me too."

Milton got to work, inspecting the situation, checking measurements and angles, procuring necessary leveraging implements, then getting the boys in position with them.

"Have any of you fellas ever heard of *Aesop's Fables*?" he asked as he worked.

"No."

"They're great stories. You want to hear one?"

"Sure!" Jacko and Pauly exclaimed. They clapped their hands and giggled with anticipation.

Everyone likes a good story.

Chapter Nine

"So, do you think Pappy's smart?"

Buddy and Oke were winding their way along the Loop Trail. Oke was making small talk.

"Are you kidding?!" Buddy exclaimed. "Of course, he is! He reads encyclopedias in his hot bathtub, for goodness sake. He knows everything!"

"Yeah, I know. But, well –"

"SHH!!" Buddy said. He raised his oversized paw and focused down the trail. He crouched. He looked to Oke.

"What? You can't crouch either?"

Oke shrugged. "I can try."

Buddy looked at his legs, and whispered, "No. Just stay real still. I think I saw something up ahead."

They watched, and then they could see them: a procession of raccoons.

They were being unruly and boisterous and using inappropriate language. It appeared they were returning from a fruitful pillage.

"Shhhh."

The raccoons passed by, not fifty feet away but unable to detect them through the jungle growth. It was thick and impenetrable here, except along the trails.

"That must be the South Trail that King Ambrosius told us about," Oke said.

"Right, which means we're almost there, to the Lodge."

They looked at each other.

"Come on," Buddy said. He led the way, easily following the scent of the new raccoons. "They smell like grits, sausage, and cinnamon buns," he said. "Must have been a good haul."

There was no hurry now. The scent of raccoons, grits, sausage, and cinnamon buns would lead them directly there.

"Keep your eyes peeled."

"Check."

Buddy noticed movement out of the corner of his eye, and he looked up in the trees to see two whippoorwills fly over and perch on a branch. They sat there nonchalantly.

He kept his eye on them a minute, then said, "What are you guys doing up there?"

"We're roosting. What do you think we're doing?"

"No, you're not. I just saw you land there a minute ago. And you're whippoorwills. You're nocturnal. Everyone knows that."

"No, we're not."

"Oh, right," Buddy said. "Sure." He paused. "You're not spying on us, are you?"

"Huh? Oh, no. Just roosting."

The two birds looked at each other and yawned.

Ho, ho, hum.

"Hmph," Buddy said. "Roosting, my foot."

"Yeah," Oke agreed. "Roosting, his foot."

"So," Buddy said after they'd gone a ways, "you believe those two?"

"Not likely," Oke shrugged. "They looked like they were up to something, that's for sure."

Slowly, cautiously, and with abundant awareness, they traversed the ever-darkening, ever-narrowing trail. The jungle seemed to press in on them. Light from the moon barely eked through.

"So, how are donkeys for night vision?"

"I don't know," Oke said.

"Can you see that white orchid on that big tree branch over there?"

Oke looked where Buddy was pointing, and said, "What tree branch?"

Buddy sighed.

"All right. Just stay close."

"Check."

A while later, Buddy raised his paw. They moved off to the side of the trail.

"That's gotta be it," Buddy said.

"It's gotta be," Oke agreed.

They looked around.

It was a cavernous opening in the trail with a high canopy overhead. On the far end of the vestibule was a small, dark hole burrowed into an impregnable wall of greenery. Standing in front of it were two guards, holding clubs in their human-like hands.

"So what do we do now?" Oke whispered.

"I suppose we need a plan."

"Well," Oke noted, "I can tell you right now that part of that plan will not include getting me through that hole."

"Yeah," Buddy said. "I can see that. Which means –"

"Which means if you're goin' in, you're goin' in alone."

"Yeah," Buddy said. "That's what it looks like, doesn't it? I wonder if there's another entrance."

Oke shrugged. "King Ambrosius didn't mention it. He would have mentioned it, wouldn't he?"

"I guess. He said it was impregnable."

"It sure looks impregnable," Oke said, looking at the tiny hole. "You're gonna have a hard time getting through that thing." He sighed. "Look, Buddy. If you don't want to do it, I understand. This might be asking too much."

"No," Buddy said. "I'll do it, but let's think about this for a minute first. We need to make a plan."

"Right," Oke said. "A plan. We need to come up with a plan."

They stared at the hole, then looked at each other, then around at the surrounding forest.

"Yep," Buddy said. "A plan. We need a plan."

*   *   *

It's tough being Boss.

Not like the Big Boss, the Pooba; but even on a smaller scale, being a regular old street boss can be tedious. No one knows like a street boss what it's like to keep a whole gang of raccoons in line. And one of the things it requires is plenty of rest – opportunity for rejuvenation – and that would include a proper amount of "me" time.

"Ah, dames. Dames, dames, dames."

Sonny was propped against a tree trunk, slouched, a pot of leftover mac and cheese on his stomach. A restless sleep disturbed his dreams.

"Why, Sonny! You're so big and strong! Oooo, Sonny. Oo, baby! Oh, my!"

Is Sonny all right?

Yo. It must'a been da mac and cheese; gives him vivid dreams.

Yeah. It happens every time.

"Oh, Sonny! How did you get so strong?!"

"It ain't nut'n, baby. Come on over hea, and give your big daddy ano'da hug."

Should we wake him up?

Sometimes he gets mad if we do.

"Oh, Sonny! You make me laugh. You're so funny – and strong!"

*   *   *

"Yo, Milton. Dat was a good idea ta help dat be'ya back d'ea."

"Ya got dat right. Dis honey is da best! And she says she has a whole tree full of it!"

"See? You never know what good can come from lending a hand to another. It can be good to help out others, can't it?" Milton smirked.

"Are ya kiddin' me?! I love dis Kaa'ma t'ing."

"Are ya kiddin' us?! We love dis Kaa'ma t'ing."

*   *   *

"Yo, baby. Why don't ya give your big daddy a nice, long, back rub?"

"Sure, honey pot."

Honey pot? Do I smell honey?

Sonny's eyes popped open.

He noticed all the faces staring back at him, and he scowled. He sat up and looked around.

"Where da dang-ding-dong you goofballs been?"

They all looked at each other, and Jacko said, "We got honey." He dipped a finger and licked it.

"Honey?" Sonny sat up a little more.

"Dat's right," Pauly said. "We got honey from da be'ya."

"Wha'd'ya talkin' about?" Sonny said, obviously flummoxed. "You's tellin' me ya got da honey from da be'ya?"

"Dat's right," Jacko said. "From – da – be'ya."

Sonny's eyes went to Milton.

"And dis one gots somet'in' ta do wid dat?"

"Ya got dat right, Sonny boy," Pauly said, dipping his whole hand in the pot. "And da be'ya said we can have more anytime we want … quantities limited."

Pauly held the pot out, and Sonny leaned in for a dip.

"Mmmm. Honey's my favoritest of all."

"Dat's right," Pauly said. "Honey and dames. Dames and honey."

As one, all three raccoons repeated the words: "Honey and dames. Dames and honey."

They high-fived, then licked their fingers.

Sonny set the pot down, and Milton went in for his own dip.

"Mmmm," he said.

"Mm-mm," the others agreed. "Mm-mm-mm."

"So, how'd you muttonheads pull dis off, anyways?"

"It's all t'anks ta Milton d'ea," Jacko said.

"Oh?"

"Dat's da trut'," Pauly said. "Good old Milt da Stilt."

"Yeah!" Jacko repeated, punching his fist in the air. "Milt da Stilt!"

"What's dat s'posed ta mean?" Sonny asked. "Milt da Stilt?"

The boys shrugged. "It rhymes."

"I guess it's okay," Sonny said. "Milt da Stilt. Dat'll be your name from now on. Ya hea?"

"Sure," Milton said. "It makes me sound like I'm tall."

Everyone nodded. And dipped.

"So, how'd ya do it? Wid da be'ya?"

Milton shrugged, and said, "We just helped one of God's creatures in their time of need."

"Huh?'

Pauly interjected, "We helped da be'ya out'a da be'ya trap."

"Da trap? Why'd ya do dat for?"

"Because," Milton replied, "we should all be prepared to help others whenever we are presented an opportunity to do so."

"But," Sonny stammered, "da be'ya ain't a raccoon."

"Well," Milton said, glancing at the boys, "I'm not ... I'm not ... " He took a deep breath. "Well, I'm not a raccoon either."

Sonny stared at him a minute. His lip began to curl, his teeth to bare.

With a sheepish smile, Milton gingerly pushed the honey pot towards him.

"More honey?"

Sonny had never, in his whole life, been more perplexed. Something was definitely wrong here, but he couldn't quite put his human-like finger on it.

"Uhhhhh."

"Yes?"

"Uhhhhhh ... I'm gonna have ta t'ink about dis one."

"That's fine," Milton said. "Take all the time you want."

"Yeah. I t'ink I will," Sonny replied, eyeing Milton suspiciously.

*   *   *

It had taken some amount of discussion, the plan.

"What do you mean, you'll dress up like a raccoon?"

"You know. I just rub some of that black dirt there around my eyes, like a mask, and hunch over ... like a big raccoon."

"A really *big* raccoon," Oke noted. "Look," he said, "we don't want to be hasty. We don't even know if they've got him in there or not."

"Shh," Buddy suddenly said. "Did you hear that?"

They looked toward the trail, and – and they stared in disbelief, watching as three raccoons sauntered around the bend, carrying bags loaded with plunder; and by the time they realized it was too late – it was.

Their eyes grew wide at the sight of Milton, sauntering along with the others.

There was no time left to plan, only time to act, except –

"Nobody move a muscle."

They turned to see several armed raccoons facing them. No! More of them to the left. And more! To the right!

The leader, with long black hair, menacingly smacked his club against his human-like hand.

Buddy prepared himself for a scrap just as he caught a glimpse of Milton, disappearing into the dread, execrable hole burrowed into the impregnable wall of greenery.

Then the lights went out.

*   *   *

Oke saw it coming, the cowardly surprise attack on his friend, but there was little he could do. But do something he did, and it was much more than anyone could have expected. It was true, the raccoons had fought off many an invader in their days. Never had they confronted one like this, though, one so well equipped to deliver such a sound and thorough thrashing.

Even before Buddy went down, Oke had sprung into action, descending into a frenzied rage. The forest had never witnessed such a display of clobbering and stomping and kicking. One after another, the raccoons charged, and Oke would send them soaring. One of them tried to get him in a headlock, but he slammed him against a tree. Once, twice, and Oke's victim cried out in pain.

It took the raccoons a few minutes to figure out that the back end of a donkey is the business end *and* that Oke had an uncanny ability to point that baleful weapon in ever-changing, unpredictable directions.

Another tried for his oversized head, and Oke easily swatted him away, sending him tumbling down the hill into the moccasin-infested swamp. Cries of panic and agony filled the air.

Down the trail the raccoons retreated under the withering, unstoppable advance.

They regrouped and attacked, but the donkey was too strong, too wieldy and powerful. Any raccoon daring to come near him got kicked or stomped. Screams of pain could be heard from all quarters. Reinforcements were called in, but Oke dominated. One after another, they fell to dainty but lethal hooves.

But even the toughest and most efficient of donkeys grow weary at some point. He gasped for air, but his determination would not falter.

Branches cracked with the weight of flying bodies, and Oke fought on.

But there were too many of them. Perhaps King Ambrosius was right; it was a fool's mission. He thought of Buddy, and he thought of Star, his pal, and Annie and Grandma, and even Pappy.

They were waiting for us! Oh, the deviousness of it all!

He kicked one in the stomach – *OOF* – sending him soaring into the brush.

It was those two birds! I knew they were trouble!

Down the trail they fought. Beyond the bounds of the hammock and into the piney woods, the battle raged. It was an epic onslaught, but there could be only one outcome, especially after the raccoons discovered every donkey's point of vulnerability: yes, the dive bomb attack from above.

To the trees the rioters went, swinging down on him from above, taking turns leaping onto Oke's extra broad, battleship-sized back. One after another, they clobbered him over the head.

The donkey has the hardest of heads and the sturdiest of bodies, but, finally, Oke's body did falter.

He stumbled, and the raccoons swarmed. Taking him down, they continued the onslaught as Oke tried futilely to fight them off. He lay prone on his side, struggling and snapping at them with his dull, non-threatening, grazer's teeth.

The last thing he saw was a grinning raccoon and a rioter's club.

Chapter Ten

Milton had never imagined such a place. It reminded him of St. Peter's Cathedral, as he imagined it from Annie's books. High above, however, where the dome would be, there was open air, so instead of Michelangelo's interpretation of what God might be, it was God's interpretation of His own creation.

A star-spangled dome.

Raccoons, different gangs, were still arriving with their nightly dues to be shared and sampled by all. There would be a vote by the Council as to whose plunder was most full of wonder. That gang would be awarded the Order of the Loot, and they would be celebrated by all and get their pick of all the best stuff.

According to the boys, the proceedings would be coming up soon.

Everyone was impressed with the new arrival, Milt the Stilt, having heard of his skills and unique talents – most everyone, anyway. Some were not impressed at all, such as Mac Slade and his cohorts.

No street gang in all the Prairie District received the Order of the Loot more often than they, but it was understandable, since their street happened to be Main Street, where all the restaurants were. It was also the biggest gang, by far.

Milton did not like the way the Mainstreeters were looking at him.

"So, what do they call us?" he asked.

"We're da Grassylaners," Jacko said. "It ain't da best duty, but it's better d'an da Coivy-doit-roaders. Dey got it da toughest, d'ose guys. Da houses on da coivy doit road belongs ta da doit farmers, and dey don't waste nut'n. Do dey, Pauly?"

"Ya got dat right," Pauly agreed. "I feel lousy for d'ose guys."

"Is it just the Curvy-dirt-roaders you feel sorry for?" Milton asked. "Or the dirt farmers too?"

The boys looked at each other, and together, they said, "Uh … bot', I guess."

Milton thought he was making progress with these two.

It was a raucous party. Milton had never seen anything like it.

When they had said women would be here, for some reason Milton had expected women like Grandma and Aunt Charlotte. People women, not raccoon women.

He had discovered that they were not the same, and that was true in many ways, starting with no cookies. None of the raccoon women knew the first thing about baking or cooking or anything else. They were just raccoons, like the others, except they were female. Most of the guys called them dames, but they used other words as well, words Milton had never heard.

He would ask, "What's that word mean?"

"A dame."

Or, "What's that word mean?"

"A dame."

There were lots of words for raccoon dames, Milton had discovered.

One of the raccoons, Milton noticed, called one of the dames one of those words, and she punched him right in the stomach. All the other raccoons laughed and drank and carried on. Milton was still having trouble with the raccoon's sense of humor. It seemed the worse the thing that happened to a raccoon, or anyone else, the funnier it was.

Milton asked about the wives and families of the raccoons.

They all just waved their hands, and said, "Get out'a hea."

In the center of the impressive hall, with the sky looking in from the heavens, was a large, flat stone. It stood out from everything else, centered as it was on the starry dome above.

"What's that for?"

"What's what for?" Pauly asked.

"That big stone in the center of the hall."

"Oh, dat's da alt'a."

"The altar?"

"Dat's right," Sonny said, distracted by a lovely young dame who was feeding him grapes from one of the night's raids. "Dat's da alt'a. You know, for da sacrificin' and all."

"Sacrificing?" Milton asked with a gulp.

"Dat's right," Jacko said. "We don't have one every night. Just sometimes, like, when da opportuni-tity presents itself."

Milton looked at the altar. He got a bad feeling.

He was actually having several bad feelings by this time, especially with the way the Mainstreeters kept leering at him.

Milton noticed some raccoons entering the Great Hall from another room. They were wearing tall, furry hats of many shapes and sizes on their heads, and they all held staffs in their ferret-like hands. They followed one another onto the wide podium and took their seats.

"Is it starting?" Milton asked. "The proceedings?"

"Dat's right," Jacko said. "Dey say it's gonna be a big show tonight."

"I can't wait," Pauly said. "It's been a long time since we got da Order 'a da Loot."

Sonny smiled and said to the fair dame, "How's about a back rub, baby, so's ta loosen me up for my big speech?"

"Sure theeng, beeg boy," the fair dame, Consuelo, replied.

Milton took it all in. This was the part he was waiting for, the proceedings. The rest of the raccoons found their seats, and everyone started to settle down.

One of the raccoons on the podium, wearing a tall red hat with a cameo brooch pinned to it, stepped up to the rostrum. He took up the gavel and rapped it three times.

"Order, order! Call to order!"

Milton watched with fascination as two rows of raccoons entered the hall. Leading them were flagbearers. They proceeded down the aisle towards the podium. Then the two rows split off and took their places on either side.

All grew quiet.

Then the tall red hat announced, "All rise for the Grand Pooba!"

Milton did as the others and stood, but he couldn't see over everyone.

Jacko picked him up and set him on his shoulder.

Milton had never witnessed such pomp or circumstance. It reminded him of the coronation of the Queen of England!

In strode the Grand Pooba: a giant of a raccoon with a scarred, grizzled face. On his head was the tallest, wooliest hat of all, and attached to the front of it was a strange symbol Milton had never seen before. The Grand Pooba appeared to be of a grave and imperturbable demeanor. He strode across the stage in a detached, obdurate manner. In his hand was the grandest staff of all, and attached to the end was some kind of jewel, emitting a greenish-yellowish hue.

Slowly, he took his position behind the rostrum. Then he gazed out over the gathered and nodded deeply. Everyone sat back down.

"We have reason for celebration tonight," he stated loudly, for all to hear. Obviously, he was from Virginia, or possibly Carolina. Milton thought he sounded like Cousin Vicki, who was from Virginia and spoke with the most soothing tone and inflection.

He paused often in his speech.

"Our coffers are full ... and we are grateful to ourselves for that. Havoc was truly done tonight ... and we theahfore dedicate it to the Gods of Disorder and Mayhem."

A mumbling coursed through the crowd.

"Tonight, we will celebrate," he drawled, "but first we must attend to necessary business. First on that list is the Order of the Loot, which, as we might all surmise, will go to the Grassy Lane Gang. I think we all agree that theah contribution tonight was extra-ordinary, not only in quality but in scope. An entire chicken coop they cleaned out! Theahfore," Pooba declared, "let's heah a big raccoon cheah for the Grassy Lane Gang!!"

Pooba led the applause as everyone's eyes in the hall turned to them: Sonny, Pauly, Jacko, Milton, and the other Grassylaners.

The applause subsided, and Pooba rapped his staff on the stage.

"With this pronouncement," he declared, "you raccoons of the Grassy Lane Gang, tonight is yours! You are heah-by deemed 'Raccoons of the hour,' and with that lofty designation, you are entitled to the pick of the spoils!"

All the raccoons in the hall chanted, "Pick of the spoils! Pick of the spoils!"

All grew quiet again.

"If there are any who disagree with this decision by the Council, step forward now."

Everyone's eyes went to a big, black-haired raccoon named Mac Slade, the leader of the Mainstreeters.

He stepped forward, and in a calloused, Mississippi possibly Alabama twang, he said, "I do. I challenge th' decision!"

Milton, who was sitting in Pauly's lap, noticed some of the raccoons were rolling their eyes.

Pauly said, "Slade always challenges da decision if it's not for his Mainstreeters."

There were mumblings through the crowd, but Pooba settled them down with his outstretched staff.

Sighing grandly, he drawled, "Go on and tell us, Broth'a Slade. What is it this time?"

Mac Slade stepped forward. Jacko had told Milton that he had been gunning for the Grand Pooba job for years now. Mac Slade had a way of speaking so that no matter what he was saying, it looked like he was sneering.

"Yeah, that's right. We, the Mainstreet Gang, are all thankful to th' Grassylaners for th' fresh eggs they delivered tonight." He sighed. "Except for one thing."

He paused, Milton thought, for effect.

"Go on, Broth'a Slade," Pooba finally said. "What is it?"

Mac Slade wheeled on his heel, pointed his finger right at Milton, and declared, "Except we have it on good authority that *that*," he shook his finger accusingly, "is *not* a raccoon! He's an imposter! It is an affront to th' Lodge! And th' Code! An affront, I say!!"

A gasp went up from the crowd. All eyes went to Milton, who got a really, really bad feeling this time.

There was an uproar, and he looked to his friends. They seemed as shocked as he was.

"Yo!" Sonny declared, getting to his feet. "Now, just hold on a minute hea." He bared his teeth at Mac Slade.

Milton looked around. There were lots of bared teeth, directed at him!

Pooba was banging on the rostrum with his gavel, but the crowd remained in a bustle.

"Order! Order!" he shouted. He banged harder. "ORDER! ORDER!"

Finally, the crowd settled down.

All eyes, however – and bared teeth – remained fixed on Milton. He looked to Jacko and Pauly. They appeared kind of nervous too. He looked to Sonny, who looked angry, but no one said anything.

Pooba looked out over the crowd at Milton, and said, "Step forward, fellow raccoon."

"May I approach as well, Your Bigness?" Sonny asked.

Pooba nodded. All watched in silence as Milton and Sonny approached the rostrum. Pooba looked down at Milton, as if studying him.

"What is your name?" he asked.

"M-Milton."

"Milton what?"

"Milton," he stammered. "Milton the … the ferret."

Another gasp went up.

"A ferret?!" The crowd exclaimed. "What's a ferret?!"

"Your Bigness!" Sonny shouted over the clamor. "Your Bigness! I gots somet'in' ta say!"

Pooba banged the gavel until there was silence.

"Go on, Broth'a Butz," he said.

"It's like dis," Sonny said. "Da kid hea's all right. Dat's right, he ain't a raccoon, but we couldn't 'a got d'ose eggs wid'out 'im. Why, ya should'a seen da little guy, haulin' dem big beauties out one at a time. And did he do it for hisself? No, he did not. He did it for us!" Sonny looked around, specifically to Mac Slade, and added, "For *all* of us!"

Mac Slade got to his feet, and shouted, "So what?! He ain't a raccoon! It's th' code! Are you sayin' th' code ain't right? Is that what you're sayin'?"

Milton looked up to Sonny, and he could tell he was getting mad.

"No," Sonny said. "Dat's not what I'm sayin', you doity … well, I'm just sayin' d'ere's gotta be some kind'a wiggle room in da Code. What about dem boids? Dey ain't raccoons nei'da, and we associate wid dem."

"That don't count," Mac Slade said. "They just work for us. We got a deal with them."

"Well d'en, why can't we make a deal wid Milt da Stilt hea?"

"Milt … the Stilt?" Pooba asked. "What is that supposed to mean?"

Sonny shrugged. "It rhymes."

A wave of moans and snickers passed through the crowd.

"Now, ever'one just hold onto yer knickers a minute!" Mac Slade said, getting his hackles up. "That ain't th' point. Don't ye get it? This here's sacred ground. That's why ye don't see th' whippoorwills here, do ye? That's b'cause this here, the Lodge, is sacred ground! This – is – the – Lodge. The Raccoon Lodge! Just look!" he cried, pointing to the badly written and spelled banner behind the podium. "It's our motto! It's our creed!"

All eyes went to the sign: "Raccoons good. Everyone else stinks."

It seemed pretty clear, particularly to Milton.

He had never felt anything like it before, this uncertainty, and even fear. How many times had his heart raced tonight for fear of some terrible fate: the barn owl swooping down and missing him by inches; then that succeeding moment when he realized he was perilously entwined with a cold, slithery Bundy Mac; or discovering there was a skunk within squirting range; and of course, the run-in with the moccasin.

It still gave him shivers to think of that, but his buddies, Sonny, Jacko, and Pauly, had come to his rescue. Now, Sonny was there for him once again. Milton could see some of the raccoons were on Mac Slade's side, and he did not want to think about what might become of him if they prevailed.

Yes, everyone had been correct when they told him it was a dangerous world out here. Now Milton knew just what they meant. But caution is not built into a ferret, and those ancient genes from some prehistoric ferret – possibly a hundred feet tall and called a Ferretyrannosaurus Rex – reared itself inside him and reminded him that ferrets are fearless.

The gathered mumbled among themselves as Pooba considered the opposing arguments.

He raised his staff for silence. He looked down at Sonny and Milton with a stern expression.

"It is indeed an affront to the Lodge, the District, and all of Raccoondom that one who is not a raccoon stands in the Lodge, side by side with us, the Loyal Broth'ahood of Chaos and Prank. Broth'a Slade is indeed correct," Pooba declared. "It is an affront!"

Sonny started to protest, but Pooba raised his staff.

"The strictures came to us thousands of years ago, and we must abide by them. None but raccoon shall be permitted within the walls of the Lodge. All others must be summarily –"

"BUT!" Sonny shouted, so all could hear. "What about da honey?!"

Honey?

All motion and sound ceased. Everyone froze to their seats.

"Dat's right! Honey! My favoritest of all!" Sonny declared, pulling his pants up a little. He looked around at the crowd. "Da honey! Who do ya t'ink got us dat honey we brought back tonight?"

Honey?

Silence reigned. Mouths watered.

"And who do ya t'ink we owe for dat?" Sonny concluded. "Why, my little pal hea, Milt – da – Stilt."

Milton had never been so moved, or felt so honored.

"And dat's not all," Sonny continued. "He got us a deal! For unlimited honey!" A gasp arose and the beginnings of a cheer, but Sonny quickly corrected, "Oh, now wait a minute d'ea. Da be'ya said *limited quantities*, so just be aware – limited quantities." He looked to Milton, and said, "Right?"

"Right."

Pooba stared, mouth agape.

Then he licked his lips and said so all could hear, "All in favor of allowin' the scrawny 'raccoon' within the walls of the Lodge, say, 'Aye.'"

Most everyone said AYE!!

"And those against?"

NAY!! The Mainstreeters, mostly, shouted along with a variety of catcalls, boos, and hisses.

"The vote carries," Pooba declared in his slow, Virginia drawl. "Now," he said, "wheah is that beautiful, scrumpdillyicious honey pot?"

Milton looked to Sonny, who said, "Come on, kid. Let's get Pooba some 'a dat honey."

"Right," Milton said. "I wouldn't mind another dip myself."

"Me nei'da," Sonny replied, patting him on the back.

*   *   *

Even among raccoons, there are unscrupulous sorts.

"Hea, hea, hea, hea, hea. Jest look at 'em, dippin' in their honey pot, makin' light 'a the whole thing."

Mac Slade was talking with his men – his raccoons – all of them watching and glaring at the Grassylaners, acting all high and mighty over there in the box seats with all their honey, eggs, and dames.

"So, what're we gonna do, boss?"

Mac slicked his long, black hair back and grinned.

"It don't matter none no-how. They're gonna git theirs."

"Really? How?"

"Let's just say a little birdie told me sump'n. Sump'n very interestin'."

"Really, boss?"

"Yeah. Really."

*   *   *

After everyone had had their fill – to the sounds of bad music played by inept, human-like hands on broken and trashed instruments – last minute preparations were underway for the big show. Everyone took their seats, the Grassylaners in the box seats, loaded to overflowing with loot and dames.

The moon came into view over the sky dome, looming so that the Lodge lit up almost like daytime.

The percussion section provided a soft drumming: *tchh-ik-a-tchh-CLUNK-tchh-ik-a-tchh-DINK.*

Some of the raccoons, dressed in flowing, recycled clothing from a generation of garbage cans, began a slow dance around the large, flat stone. Milton got that feeling again. He didn't know why. No, he knew why: they said it was the sacrificial stone.

Milton didn't really think he was up for a sacrifice.

The tempo picked up. The dancers moved faster with it, waving their arms around in the air and chanting unintelligibly.

All eyes, Milton noticed, were fixed on the far entrance. Then there was a rustling of greenery, and one of the tall-hats appeared, his staff held high. He was wearing a red cape with that strange symbol on it: part square, part circle, part trapezoid. As he proceeded, he moved the staff back and forth. Another tall hat followed. Then came two raccoons, one right after the other, wearing what looked like togas. They appeared to be carrying something on their shoulders. Yes, it was the end of a pole – a long, stout pole.

There was something, or someone, tied to the stout pole, and holding up the other end were two more bearers.

Who are these ... animals?! Milton wondered. Then he remembered: there was a reason Pappy didn't like raccoons.

Milton looked at his friends, the Grassylaners. He wondered how this could be?

Oh, the horror. Whoever it was, was suspended from the stout pole, tied to it by the legs. He could see it was someone big ... and brown ... with a thick, black snout.

A thick black snout?!

Milton's beady eyes grew several sizes.

He gasped in horror, and he swallowed hard.

It was Buddy. They had Buddy!

BUDDY!!

Milton was beside himself. His heart seemed to have stopped. His mouth was dry, and he thought he might be sick.

IT'S BUDDY!! THEY'RE GONNA SACRIFICE BUDDY!

The crowd was silent as the procession made its way to the large, flat stone.

How can this be?!

Buddy seemed confused. It looked like he'd been beaten up. Milton never thought he'd ever witness it, but Buddy looked scared. Yes, he looked scared. It tore at Milton's insides, and he wondered if all this had something to do with him.

Oh, no! It's all my fault! It's ALL my fault! Buddy came looking for me! For ME!! Oh, the travesty!

"Hey," Sonny said. "Ain't dat da big dog from up at da house?"

The other Grassylaners looked, and said, "Yeah. It is, ain't it?"

They all looked to Milton and he to them.

Chapter Eleven

A cricket chirped.

Otherwise, quiet.

It was a bug, something small, maybe a fly, a mosquito, that finally roused Okey Donkey.

An incessant buzzing in his ear.

All was black. Slowly, his eyes opened. He looked around. Strange, unfamiliar objects. It was dark and dank. It smelled musty and old. The rot of ages. At first, he simply lay there. He didn't know where he was. He didn't know who he was. Or even if he was.

Had he died and gone to Heaven? Or that other place?

Do donkeys go there?

It all seemed so strange and otherworldly: sights, smells, sounds.

Pine needles. Yes. Something familiar.

He felt pains throughout his entire consciousness, sharp and dull ones, throbbing and stinging ones, but they seemed far away. He listened to the cricket chirping, and he looked upward into a tangled morass. Specks of light showed through. He struggled, racking his brain, trying to figure out what was happening to him.

The buzzing was becoming a nuisance. He tried lifting his head, but bolts of pain shot through his body. He released an involuntary whine and took deep, agonizing breaths.

"Are you okay?"

Huh? Who's that?

Oke moved his head, just enough to look around.

Yes, he was remembering now. The forest. He was in the forest. The pine forest. They had fought all the way down the trail, all the way to the fringes of the pine forest.

"Over here," the voice said.

Oke managed to move his head a little, and what he saw almost made him laugh.

It was all coming back to him now, in flashes. They had been off to save Milton from the raccoons, he and Buddy. And Buddy was hurt. Yes, he was injured, probably captured. There had been a fight. Yes, the fight. A horrible fight. It was all coming back to him now.

"Are you okay?"

Oke couldn't hold back the laugh. It hurt all over, but the sight of a tortoise looking down at him with a concerned expression was so comical, he couldn't help it.

"I don't know," Oke gasped. He lifted his head and lay it back down. "Just give me a minute."

"Oh, all I've got is time. Name's Larry, by the way."

"Nice, *cough*, to meet you."

"You think you can get up?"

"I ... I don't know," Oke said. "Let me see if can get the front up. Then I'll let you know."

It took a couple of agonizing tries, but on the third effort, he managed to get onto his front knees. He grimaced and tried to breathe, but it hurt.

Then something caught his eye, and at that same moment, Larry said, "This is my roommate, Spud Grant."

Oke was just about to say hello to Spud Grant but then realized Spud Grant was not another tortoise. He was a monstrous-sized, diamondback rattlesnake!

And Oke was on his feet, just like that.

He was wobbly, and fear gushed from his eyes, but he was ready. At a moment's notice, he could be gone! *Whoosh!*

The only word to escape him, however, was "G-a-a-ack!"

Oke's eyes darted between Larry and Spud Grant, the gargantuan rattlesnake, coiled and leering. The snake's tongue flicked in and out creepily and insidiously.

"Howdy," he said. "I'm from down south a ways. Nice to meet ya." He looked at Larry and snickered knowingly. "Hope ya don't mind if I don't shake your hand."

"Uh," Oke stammered. "Uh ... no. I don't suppose so."

"Spud here's a real cut-up," Larry said.

"So I see," Oke replied, eyeing Spud nervously. "But I gotta ask," he said, glancing between them, "You say you two are ... roommates?"

"Sure," Larry said. "We get along fine, in our burrow. He helps me out. I help him out. It works out fine. It's not like he's gonna swallow me whole." Larry shrugged. "Nobody bothers us."

"No, I don't suppose they do," Oke said.

"Yeah," Spud agreed. "Larry snores, but I don't mind, and he doesn't get mad when I forget to wipe my feet."

Oke looked curiously at the humongous, viperous serpent. Spud laughed, with a hiss.

"Ha-ss, ha-ss, ha-ss. That's a good one, isn't it? Wipe my feet? I don't have any feet! Get it?!"

"Uh ... yeah," Oke said. "That's a ... good one."

"Spud's a real joker," Larry interjected. "Always joking around."

"Not everyone would say that," Spud noted. "But, yeah. I am a funny guy." He looked sideways at Oke. "Don't ya think?"

"Oh!" Oke replied. "Yes. Yes, I do."

Just what I need, a comedian rattlesnake.

"It's all the talk, you know," Larry said.

"What?"

"You! You and that big dog. And that scrawny, raccoon-looking thing."

"That's Buddy and Milton. Me and Buddy were on our way to save him, but the raccoons got the jump on us."

"That's what we heard," Larry said. "News travels fast in the forest, even at night."

"So I see," Oke replied. "And you say everyone's talking about it?"

"Yep."

"Hm," Oke said. "So, did you hear what happened to Buddy?"

"The big, brown dog?"

"Yeah."

Larry grew somber. "All we know is that they took him inside the Lodge."

"The Lodge," Oke repeated with a donkey snarl. "I've gotta go save him. Save *them*!"

"You can't save them," Larry said, looking to Spud Grant. "No one leaves the Lodge once they enter." He paused. "Not alive anyway."

The words cut through Oke like a knife.

"I don't care," he said. "I'm going." With that, he started off up the trail.

"Well, hold on a minute," Larry said. "Don't be in such a big hurry. Maybe we can help."

Oke looked at the odd pair and shook his head.

"I don't think so. Anyway, I can't ask you to do that."

"No," Larry corrected. "You can't afford *not* to."

"I suppose you're right." Oke sighed. "Well, come on, then." He turned to head up the trail leading into the hammock.

"Uh, hold on a minute, there," Spud spoke up. "You think I can 'aaa, get a lift?"

Oke's jaw dropped. He felt a wave of true, bone-tingling dread shiver up his spine. He stared, mortified, at the giant snake, at the perpetually testy, not funny-looking at all, cold-blooded eyes staring back at him.

"Uhhhh," he sighed. "Uhhhh … are you gonna be able to … hold on all right?"

"No prob," Spud replied. "I've got a surprisingly good grip, and you've got a mighty broad back."

"Great," Oke mumbled to himself. "A good grip and a broad back."

"What did you say?" Spud asked.

"Oh, nothing," Oke sighed.

"All rightee, then," Larry said. "I guess I'll meet you guys there."

"Right," Oke sighed. "You can meet us there, uh … whenever. Right?"

"It's the way of the tortoise," Larry replied with a philosophical pose. "I'll be there when I get there."

"Great," Oke mumbled to himself. Then he looked to the king-sized rattlesnake and cringed; and with a tremulous sigh, he said, "I guess you should … uh … climb on board, then?"

Without a doubt, it was the creepiest moment of Oke's life.

And off they went, miniature donkey and colossal rattlesnake, quickly leaving Larry behind.

*　　　*　　　*

Back at the Lodge, everything was going along swimmingly.

Of all the animals in the animal kingdom, raccoons despise dogs the most. As far as the average raccoon is concerned, dogs are there only to ruin their fun, and not necessarily by physically beating them up but by raising a ruckus and bringing human attention to their "labors of love" – which could be summed up as rioting, raiding, and looting.

It does not bother raccoons that they are personae non gratae: from the reception they receive wherever they go, to those signs placed along the roadsides at the edge of the woods, saying, "No Hunting (except for raccoons)." Of course, something like a sign would never hinder anyone with an ingrained sense of duty and commitment, like a raccoon. Anyway, it was the humans who put the signs there, and, as everyone knows, humans are the lowest form of life – at least from a raccoon's perspective.

It was they, the humans, who had everything raccoons wanted. Someday, according to raccoon prophesy, they themselves would take over the world – again. Then it would be them, raccoons, living in the houses and shooting at humans out by the chicken coop. It would be them, raccoons, driving cars and plowing right through families of humans out for a midnight stroll.

It was a pipe dream, of course, but one had to wonder: why else would raccoons have human-like hands if not because they were next in line for world domination? And what was the best way to set off on that long held, most desirable end? To start out small.

Not too small, for this was a big dog, and not just any big dog, but the big dog from the end of the grassy lane. He was famous among raccoons, mostly for the Great Battle of the Fence Line. Everyone knew about it for miles around, the time the big brown dog battled six dogs at once, and won. And that wasn't just any dogs, either, but those notorious Farmer Perkins's dogs, the Sinister Six, as they were known.

Now he was theirs, the big brown dog. A true prize and the first of many! Next would come the Sinister Six themselves. Oh, the glory that radiated from the eyes of the gathered as Pooba went on, describing in vaunted and vivid terms what would most certainly, someday, become reality: the day the raccoon would rule.

Buddy did not like the sound of all this. He hated the thought of raccoons living in the house. Where would his family live, Annie and the others? A rage developed inside him, but there was nothing he could do, hanging from the stout pole as he was.

His feet were starting to hurt, and it was getting hard to hold up his head so his nose didn't drag on the ground.

He could see things weren't good for him. These raccoons meant business.

Buddy chastised himself for letting them get the drop on him; but he and Oke had been surrounded. Still, what it might do to his reputation irked him.

He wondered where Oke was, and it gave him a hollow feeling inside. And, of course, there was Milton. When Buddy had come to, he had asked his captors about his friends, so they had tied his mouth shut. Buddy had bitten two of them in the process, which had made him feel a little better.

Buddy had no idea there were this many raccoons in the state, much less the township.

Of course, everything was upside down. At the moment, that was the worst part. He desperately searched the crowd for Milton, but it was hard because everything was upside down.

Finally, the big upside-down raccoon, the Grand Pooba, finished his speech.

He raised his staff and said in a soothing, Virginia drawl, "Prepare the sacrificial dog!"

Buddy couldn't believe it was happening. He didn't think anyone still held sacrifices these days.

This is crazy! And isn't it supposed to be a lamb? A sacrificial lamb?!

He was angry. Oh, he was mad, but there was nothing he could do as they carried him over to the large, flat stone.

The full moon was shining down, still ascending, not quite overhead yet.

He looked at the stone, and he could see there were ropes attached to the sides, obviously for tying him down. It terrified him, but what could he do?

Maybe, hopefully, they would untie him to get him onto it. That would be his chance. Desperately, he looked around for Milton, but it was so crowded, and everything was upside down, and –

And there he is!

There was no doubt. It was Milton, and he was looking right at him. He was sitting with the raccoons in the box seats, just looking and watching. Buddy wondered what kind of spell they had cast over him.

How, he wondered, could this be happening?

*   *   *

Milton wondered as well: how could this be happening?

"We have to help him!" he cried. "You have to do something!"

Milton noticed that Sonny and the others were, all of a sudden, hesitant to help. They just sat quietly and listened to Pooba going on about how someday the raccoon would rule the world.

Sonny wore a grim expression. He shook his head.

"I don't know, kid. Dis is a tough one. We already pushed our luck wid you. And da ceremony, it's already started. We could get in big trouble, ya know, stickin' up for a doity dog."

"Big trouble like *that*?!" Milton said, pointing at Buddy being hauled over to the large, flat stone.

The other Grassylaners gathered around and listened intently.

"Well, no," Sonny replied. "But –" He paused and grimaced. Then he sighed and grumbled, "Whatev'a." He stood up, raised his hand, and shouted, "Your Bigness! Yo! Your Bigness! I gots somet'in' ta say!"

All looked to the box seats, overflowing with Grassylaners and dames.

Pooba scowled, then he signaled the sacrifice detail to hold.

"You may speak, Broth'a Butz," he said in his easy, Virginia drawl.

Sonny appeared nervous. He took a deep breath.

"If I may, Your Bigness! I never got my speech, ya know, for da Order 'a da Loot! And it is my poi-rogative, ya know."

"It is," Pooba affirmed, looking around at the others. "But can't it wait? We're right in the middle of the sacrifice, as you can see."

"I know dat, but I t'ink da rule says I get my speech when we get our award; and I did not – get – my – speech." He crossed his arms.

Milton looked on as hope and terror mingled freely in his heart. Milton thought Buddy had spotted him, but he couldn't be sure.

It was clear Pooba was not happy with the turn of events, but he finally nodded, and said, "Your pardon, everyone, but Broth'a Butz is indeed correct." He looked to the box seats. "You have the floor, Broth'a Butz."

As Sonny made his way to the podium, Milton held his little human-like hands to his chest, and he prayed. It was all he could do, so he did it as hard as he could.

A minute later, Sonny was on the stage, at the rostrum.

*   *   *

"Yo."

It was Sonny's standard opening line, regardless of the occasion.

"Yo!" the crowd answered back. Most liked Sonny and his Brooklyn boys.

"So, da foist t'ing I gots ta do is t'ank everyone for sayin' all da nice t'ings about our eggs and honey. It was somet'in, I tell ya, watchin' da little guy haul d'ose big, delicious orbs 'a snackity-snack out da coop. He woiked his little heart out, he did." Sonny looked out into the audience, and said, "Yo, Milt da Stilt! Stand up and take a bow!"

Everyone looked to the box seats, to a tiny form perched on the edge of the railing, waving sheepishly.

"Give 'im a big hand, everyone! A big hand for my little buddy!"

Sonny led the crowd in a round of applause.

"All right, all right," he said. "Good job, Milt da Stilt. Milt da Stilt, everyone! T'ank you, Milt – da – Stilt. Now," he went on. "I just want'a say a few more words, if dat's all right wid you. I been woikin' down hea a long time, and I seen lots 'a t'ings goin' on. Now, I ain't gonna name names, but just let me say right hea, right now, dat d'ea's lots'a stuff dat goes on around hea dat ain't exactly kosher, if ya know what I mean. But I ain't gonna bring dat up. No, I'm not. And I know dat rules is rules, and customs is customs, but sometimes I t'ink it's best dat we just … uhhhh, dat we just, well, we just t'ink about one anud'a's feelin's."

A gasp arose from the crowd, then a wave of muted grumblings.

"Now, just hold on a minute, d'ea. Let me finish."

"Boo! Get off the stage!" someone yelled from the gallery.

Pooba, standing behind Sonny, raised his greenish-yellowish tipped staff, and all grew quiet again.

"T'ank you, Pooba," Sonny said. "Now, it toins out dat dis hea dog, da one from my very precinct, happens to be a close, bosom buddy of my little buddy, Milt – da – Stilt."

Sonny sensed discontent ebbing through his audience.

"Now, now," he said. "I'm just askin' for one little favor hea. Da dog hea, he was just comin' 'round ta find his little buddy, my little buddy, because he was worried about him. Don't ya see? It wasn't da dog's fault dat he ended up hea, and it wasn't good old Milt da Stilt's fault ei'da. If anyone is ta blame hea, it is me. I was da one dat broke da rules, and I want ta say right now dat I am so, so sorry. D'ea I said it. It was my fault, and I'm so, so sorry."

Sonny hung his head with contrition.

A deathly pall settled over the hall.

The moon was riding high.

Pooba stepped forward, and drawled, "Thank you, Broth'a Butz."

Sonny looked at the crowd, then over at Milton, wringing his tiny raccoon-like hands. With a heavy sigh, he started back to his seat.

"That was very well stated," Pooba said. "We all thank you for that, Broth'a Butz. Now," he said, raising his staff. "Proceed with the proceedings."

With that, the big, brown dog was lowered onto the large, flat stone. A dozen raccoons gathered around to hold him down while others untied him from the stout pole so they could fasten him to the stone, on his back, in a very unbecoming pose – for a dog especially.

*　　*　　*

"We're gonna need help."

Spud Grant shrugged his shoulders. He was half-draped over Oke's withers and mane, his head bobbing back and forth several inches behind Oke's ears as they ambled down the trail.

"I don't know about that," Spud said. "No one's gonna want to help a house animal, and, of course, there's me."

"Right," Oke said. "I suppose you have something of a … reputation."

"I do," Spud conceded. "An undeserved reputation, I might add. I mean, what's a rattlesnake supposed to do when someone is about to step on him? I mean, I could just strike, but I prefer to warn, to caution the other individual so they are aware of my presence."

Oke nodded. "I've heard Pappy say that the rattlesnake is the gentleman of snakes, just for that reason."

"Hm," Spud said. "I'd like to meet this fine fellow, Pappy, someday."

"No, you wouldn't," Oke said. "Trust me. He might say that, but it's more likely he's gonna whack you with the garden rake first, and ask questions later."

"Mm," Spud mumbled. "It's like that with lots of folks, I suppose."

"Well," Oke said. "You do look kind of scary, and you do have those giant, white fangs dripping with deadly venom."

"Yeah," Spud sighed. "I suppose I do. So," he said, "what's the plan, Stan?"

"Well, I guess we don't want a repeat of the last rescue attempt." Oke sighed. "We need some kind of help. And there's gotta be another way into the Lodge."

"Well," Spud said, "I have no doubt I can get in. How about I go in and scare everyone out and you trample them to death one at a time as they come out?"

"That sounds dangerous," Oke replied. "I don't know how many there are, but there's a lot of them, and you should have someone to cover your back. Speaking of which, there's got to be a back entrance, don't you think?"

"I don't know," Spud said. "I know me and Larry like to have a back door, you know, just in case."

"Exactly," Oke said. "Just in case."

He stopped and looked around. He sniffed at the musty, jungle air.

He looked up into the trees, and announced, "I know someone's out there, watching and listening. I've seen how it is here in the forest, but I also know how most of you forest folks feel about those scurrilous raccoons. Well, I just want you to know that one of my friends, a good boy named Buddy, and another friend named Milton, are possibly being held prisoner by the raccoons." He paused to listen.

"Hear anything?" he asked Spud Grant.

"I don't really hear that good, I gotta tell you."

Oke scowled, and spoke out again.

"Now I know what you folks – and I know you're out there – must be thinking; us two, out here in the middle of the forest, you know, together like this. But it's for a reason. Spud here, who is a very nice rattlesnake by the way, has volunteered to help me rescue my friends from the raccoons. And I know how most of you feel about the raccoons. Well, this is the time, folks! This is the moment, your chance to help turn the tables on those devilish demons!"

"Devilish demons?" Spud queried.

Oke shrugged.

"Let me try," Spud suggested.

"Go ahead," Oke said, "but ... well ... just ... go ahead."

Spud Grant raised his scaly head and hissed as loudly as he could, "Uh, hello, everyone. I think you all know who I am. Now first off, let me say I just ate a few days ago, so I am not, I repeat, not hungry! I only say this to reassure you. We are in need of assistance. My friend, Larry, some of you may know him – he's been living here forever – well, he's on his way as well, and we decided to help Oke here because we've all had it with those no account raccoons! And I know you have too! Why, who hasn't? They are rude, crude, and dare I say LEWD! Oh, my gosh! Can they be lewd!! Anyway, I know someone is listening out there, and Oke is right. Someone needs to teach them a lesson, and now is the time! We need your help to get Buddy and Milton, two very nice guys, out of there before – well, I don't even want to think about it."

Spud paused to gather his thoughts, then he concluded.

"So, come on, everyone! I know someone's listening out there! And I know you know what Oke did today! It was momentous! It was stupendous! It was .. it was ..."

"Oh, please. I can't take another word."

Oke and Spud looked upward, into the trees. Far above, barely visible in the shadows, was the great horned owl.

"Oh!" Spud and Oke exclaimed. They looked at each other, and both bowed – badly.

"Your Highness," Spud said. "We didn't know you were there."

"Obviously," King Ambrosius replied.

The king went on to say he would speak to his "minions" about it, as long as Spud Grant would shut up.

"Oh, no problem," Spud said. "Please do! Please speak to your minions!"

Then they watched as the giant bird took wing without a sound and disappeared into the star-dappled sky.

"Well," Spud said. "It can't hurt, I guess."

"No," Oke agreed. "It can't hurt. So, is he really a king? And he has minions?"

Spud shrugged. "No one really knows. Lots of disinformation campaigns out there, I hear."

"Yeah," Oke sighed. "That's what I hear too. So," he said. "Shall we proceed?"

"We shall," Spud replied, and he got all settled onto Oke's mighty broad back.

They had started down the trail again when another voice said, "Maybe I can help."

Donkey and rattlesnake turned and – horror of horrors! Only feet away! And well within squirting range!!

Stark terror emanated from their eyes, and instantly, reflexively, both shied and started to back away.

"Oh, my Lord!" the skunk said. "Do I have to go through this every time? I only squirt if I'm in danger. Am I in danger?"

Oke and Spud Grant looked to each other. They shook their heads.

A minute later, the oddest of trios proceeded down the trail.

Chapter Twelve

Buddy felt a little better, knowing that Milton had not gone to the other side. It had been a moving speech by Sonny, and Buddy had thought it might work. But alas.

So now it was up to him to save himself or die trying.

A dozen sets of human-like hands held him in place while others untied the knots holding his feet to the stout pole. He could smell their putrid, raccoon breath. Flames coursed up his spine. But he remained calm. There would only be a matter of seconds in which to make his move. Timing would be everything.

Patience. Patience. NOW!!

Buddy whipped his entire body in one direction, then instantly reversed, throwing all his weight the opposite way. Small hands grasped at him, savagely and blindly, but even for an old dog, Buddy was powerful, and he squirmed viciously. Furiously, he fought them, throwing his weight and kicking, never giving them the chance to get a grip on him.

Then he was on his feet. Human-like hands clawed at him, trying to drag him down; but he was relentless, struggling, wriggling, writhing, and twisting. Finally, he shook himself loose of the grimy grasps, and with all his might, he leaped!

He found himself free of them, those gathered at the stone, but they and others were moving in on him. There was no time! He looked around, desperate, towards the plaza entrance. He could make his escape, easily. It was right there. Then he looked to the box seats and Milton. Without hesitation, he bounded across the floor, knocking several raccoons out of the way. Then he was there, in the box seats, face to face with Milton and his gang of raccoons.

*   *   *

Milton was beside himself.

The raccoons were untying Buddy from the stout pole so they could tie him down to the stone. But what could Milton do? Nothing. And what could Sonny and the others do? Nothing.

Milton held his face in his hands and cried.

But there was a commotion down on the floor, and he opened his eyes to see a fight. Yes! Buddy was fighting them! He was trying to get away! The raccoons were in a state, trying to hold him back, but he was too strong and too fast. Before Milton knew it, Buddy had broken free, and in several bounds he was all of a sudden with him, in the box seats!

"Mmmmmm!" Buddy said, indicating his mouth.

Milton could see the Grassylaners were as shocked as he, but he didn't hesitate, and he reached up and started tugging on the strip of cloth holding Buddy's mouth shut. To his relief, Sonny reached over and yanked it off.

Raccoon and dog, mortal enemies, stared at one another. Beyond the bounds of the box seats, the other raccoons gathered, all of them baring their teeth and growling.

Milton looked to Sonny with pleading eyes.

"Sheesh, dis is gettin' old," Sonny grumbled. Then he winked at Milton, turned to his gang, and said, "Look, boys. It's all for one, and one for all, right?"

Milton could see some of the Grassylaners weren't as enthusiastic as others, but they all nodded their assent. Sonny turned to the seething mob before him.

"Now look hea, fellas," he said. "Ain't nobody takin' Milt da Stilt or his buddy, Buddy. So, hea's how it's gonna go. Me and my boys is gonna excort our friends out'a hea. I promise dey won't ev'a come back, but go we will, and ain't nobody gonna stop us, or dey will be very sorry."

A murmur passed through the crowd of incensed raccoons. They all knew that Sonny had been the Kung Fu champion, raccoon division, of the Brooklyn borough three years straight. That had been back in the day, though.

A voice shouted from the left, a distinct Mississippi twang.

"This is treason!" Mac Slade declared with an accusing finger.

"It is not!" Sonny shouted back. "Milt da Stilt is one of us! Da Grassylan'as. He's a honorary raccoon, even if he ain't one by boith! He's one of us! And I noticed ya didn't mind gobblin' up his eggs and honey! Did ya?! Remember da honey?! The DEAL for da honey? Milton hea is a poi'sonal friend 'a da be'ya, so dat might be goin' away if ya ain't careful."

"Honey?" the crowd murmured.

It was obvious to Milton that the raccoons treasured their honey.

"That don't matter!" Mac Slade shouted, his face turning red. "We're raccoons! We have the right ta sacrifice whoever we want! Any time we want!"

"Oh, yeah?" Sonny shouted back. "Den put it to a vote, why don't ya?"

With that, everyone's eyes went to Grand Pooba, who seemed undecided himself ever since the mention of the honey deal. He looked to the other tall hats, and they huddled for an impromptu meeting.

All waited, talking among themselves.

Mac glared at Sonny; Sonny at Mac.

Finally, Pooba approached the rostrum. He banged his gavel, and all grew quiet.

"It has been decided by the Council that a vote shall be held." He gazed out over the gathered, and declared, "All those for allowin' the intruders ta leave unmolested, and theahby keep the honey deal with the bear, raise your human-like hands."

Hands went up. One of the tall hats, the official Raccoon Lodge counter, made his tally.

"Very well," Pooba said. "And all opposed?"

Hands went up, and the official counter counted.

There was another discussion. Then Pooba came back to the rostrum.

With a grave countenance, he said, "Unfortunately, we have a tie."

All was silent as Pooba grimaced in thought.

"When a situation such as this arises, a tie, it is up to the Grand Pooba, who is I, to cast the decidin' vote." He paused. "I do not take this lightly, I assure you."

All grew quiet again, with scattered murmurings.

With hope, Milton looked to Sonny, who winked, and said with a sly smile, "Don't worry, little buddy. I happen ta know da Pooba loves his honey. And," he added, "he also happens ta be my bro'da-in-law – and not only dat, he owes me twenty bucks!"

Milton looked to Buddy with hope in his eyes as Pooba consulted with the other tall hats. Finally, he approached the rostrum. He held his staff tipped with the greenish-yellowish stone in front of him, and made his proclamation.

"The vote has been cast," he said. "It has been decided that the guests of the Grassylaners will be permitted to leave without further impediment."

There was a hush over the gathered, then an uproar from, primarily, Mac Slade and his Mainstreeters. It seemed there was nothing they could do, though.

Sonny looked to Milton, then to Buddy, and said, "So, d'ea ya go. Dee-mocracy in action."

"But," Milton asked, "what if the vote had gone the other way?"

Sonny shrugged. "No problem. We'd'a got ya out'a hea. I'm just glad you and da boys thought ta help out da be'ya."

Milton couldn't see how they would have gotten away. He was simply relieved it was all over. He looked to Buddy, who sat like a good boy and held out his paw for a shake.

"Thanks, Sonny," Buddy said. "I appreciate it."

"Get out'a hea," Sonny replied.

"That's what I'm planning on," Buddy said. "What do you say, Milt? Shall we head back home?"

"I thought you'd never ask," Milton replied.

A minute later, he was saying his goodbyes to Jacko and Pauly and the other Grassylaners. Then there was a sudden commotion out on the floor. It didn't look good. The Mainstreeters and others were gathering in defiance of the vote. With Mac Slade leading them, they slowly approached the box seats. No, it did not look good. They were hissing and baring their teeth and smacking clubs against human-like hands.

Slowly and menacingly, they approached.

"All right, everyone," Sonny said to the others, far outnumbered by the approaching mob, "just stick wid me. We make our stand right hea. Ba-da-bing – ba-da-bang – ba-da-boom."

"Ba-da-bing – ba-da-bang – ba-da-boom!" the Grassylaners repeated.

Milton looked at them with wonder. Every one of them, to the raccoon, was prepared for a fight, and for no other reason but to save him and Buddy – and a honey contract.

"We'll show 'em," Sonny said, wielding his own club. "We'll show dem undem-o-cratic rascals dat a friend indeed is a friend in need … uh, wait a minute –"

"A friend in need," Milton offered, "is a friend indeed."

"Right," Sonny said, winking at Milton. "T'anks, little buddy."

Milton looked around at the Grassylaners, then to Buddy, all of them ready to fight, and he knew there was only one thing to do, and that was to put up his dukes and do his best.

Most of the other raccoons had backed away, watching as the Mainstreeters advanced on the box seats. No, it did not look good for the Grassylaners, outnumbered two to one.

But then arose a riotous clamor from the far side of the hall. All eyes went to the pool parlor entrance; and to their amazement, a raccoon came soaring out, landing on his head. Then another one. And another. In turn, each got up and ran away.

All eyes trained on the pool hall to see a sight of sights; for though some had recently witnessed it close up, none had ever witnessed a donkey's hind end crashing through the wall of greenery that was the "impregnable" bulwark of the Raccoon Lodge.

No, none had ever witnessed such a thing as:

HEEEEEEEE!! HAWWWWWW!!

The shocked occupants put their hands over their ears and watched in stunned silence.

Then someone shouted, "What is THAT!!"

"It's a donkey!!" another voice shouted.

Then another: "And he's got a rattlesnake! Everybody run for it!"

"No!" Mac Slade shouted. "They can't get us all! Get 'em!"

The raccoons were hesitant, however, at the sight of the large, raging beast with a giant pit viper on its back.

HEEEEEEEE!! HAWWWWWW!!

SSSSSSSSSS!!

"GO GET 'EM!!"

Milton watched as one after another charged the donkey and rattlesnake, but were quickly vanquished. Still, more raccoons took up the challenge, charging all at once until, until –

"AHHHHHHHHHH!! He's got a skunk! He's got a skunk! Everybody run for it! Every raccoon for himself!! AHHHHHHHHHH!!"

And they all ran away, trampling each other as they crowded through the tiny vestibule in an effort to escape the most horrific of horrors.

*   *   *

A few minutes later, all was quiet in the Great Hall. There was no one else around but those in the box seats. They were chatting and dipping honey.

"So," Sonny said. "Dat was quite a show dea, Okey Donkey. Remind me nev'a to get in a dis-poote wid you."

Everyone laughed.

"But," he said, "how did yous get in da back way? Dea is no back way."

"There is now," Patty said, "thanks to Oke here and King Ambrosius, who told us of a weak spot in the Lodge's ramparts. We knew we had found it because we could hear all the commotion in here, so Oke just pointed his butt in that direction and plowed straight ahead – or straight aback."

Everyone looked to Oke with wonder and marvel.

He shrugged. "Aw, it was nothing."

"And did you all know," Buddy added, "that Oke killed a coyote once?"

"Ooooo. Impres-tive," Sonny said. "Maybe we'll make you guys honorary Grassylan'as too. Wha'd'ya fellas t'ink about dat?"

Oke and Buddy looked to Milton, who said, "Are you kidding? We'd love to have you fellas on board." He looked warily at Spud Grant, and added, "why, we'd all be Lodge brothers … right?"

"Uh, sort'a kind'a," Sonny said. "So, what's it gonna be? You fellas Grassylan'as or not?"

Buddy, Oke, Spud, and Patty looked at each other and nodded.

With that, Sonny said, "Den I hea'by deem you fellas, Buddy, Oke, Spud, and Patty, as official-type Grassylan'as."

Once everyone had had their share of honey, they all headed out, towards the big, miniature donkey-sized hole in the so-called impenetrable wall of greenery.

"Hey!" Pauly said. "Dis is kind'a like a fable, ain't it?"

"Yeah," Jacko agreed. "It is. Like, da moral of da story is ya never know what good can come from when ya lend a hand."

"You sure don't," Milton agreed.

As they were leaving, Sonny said, "Maybe we'll start our own lodge. Wha'da you fellas t'ink about dat?"

"Sounds good ta me," Jacko said.

"Yeah. Me too," Pauly replied.

Then they were gone, disappeared into the forest.

Chapter Thirteen

The sun had yet to declare its arrival. The grays and golds of dawn remained beyond the eastern horizon. The moon was big, bright, and sinking in the west. All was still on the farm.

Cock-a-doodle-done-did had yet to rouse from his slumber, but then, he wasn't much of an early riser.

Pappy, however, was, so he never counted on Cock-a-doodle-done-did. For that task, he depended on the mockingbirds and their cheery morning songs. Yes, even an old curmudgeon like Pappy could appreciate a well-performed ditty early in the morning.

But there was no song, not yet. Pappy's eyes snapped open.

He looked around. He was in his easy chair.

A scowl creased his face, but not necessarily out of anger.

"Danged dog," he mumbled.

He put on his glasses and looked at the clock on the mantle. He sighed.

"Danged old dog."

He lowered the chair and sat up. He rubbed his eyes, and slowly stood, holding his lower back as he did.

"Danged chair."

He glanced up the stairs, then he shuffled out, through the kitchen. He paused to look in the refrigerator and take a drink of orange juice right out of the bottle, then he shuffled on to the back door.

"Bad dog."

He opened the door. Without looking, he said, "Come on in, bad dog."

Kitty strutted in.

Meow.

"Oh, hi, Kitty. You seen Buddy?"

Kitty didn't answer. Pappy's brow furrowed.

"Danged dog."

Barefoot, he shuffled out to the porch and looked around. No Buddy. He was starting to get worried.

"Maybe someone else let him in," he mumbled to himself. "Buddy!" he shouted. "Hey! Buddy! Where the heck are ya?!"

No answer. No sound of padding paws. No heavy panting.

"HEY! BUDDY!"

But no big, brown dog.

"Danged dog," he grumbled. He turned to go back into the house, and something caught his eye. He looked and froze in place, his eyes like saucers.

"Dang it! The door's open!"

He dashed over to the laundry room door, burst inside, and turned on the light.

"Milton!" he shouted. "Where are you?! Are you here?!"

In a mad frenzy, he searched the room, tossing clothes and buckets and boxes aside.

"Milton!"

He pulled all the stuff from beside the washer.

"Milton!"

He pictured Annie's face. He got down on his knees and crawled into the space between the washer and the water heater.

"Milton! Are you back there?!"

He wiggled and squiggled and looked behind the washer.

"Holy, St. Pete!" he cried. "Look at all this stuff! Milton! Are you in there?!"

He started pulling things out, one after another: Davey's blue jeans, Annie's socks, Mammy's dress, and, "Why, you son of a gun! It was you that stole my overalls!" He dragged them out, and said, "Wait a minute. What's that?" He looked in the pocket, and there it was, his pocket knife, the one his grandpappy had given him.

It was a moment of mixed feelings for Pappy: joy at finding his most treasured possession, and rage at Milton for being such a thief.

"Danged … FERRET!"

With some difficulty, he wriggled his way back out of the cramped space. He stood up and looked around.

"Dang it!!"

He stood there a minute, breathing hard, thinking. Then he dashed back in the house, through the kitchen, up the stairs, into the bedroom.

Grandma was sleeping peacefully. He didn't want to give her a heart attack, so he crept up to her and shook her gently.

"Hm? What?" she asked, sleepy voiced.

"The door," Pappy said. "It was open."

Grandma's brain creaked, and her eyes popped wide. She bolted upright, her hand going for the lamp switch.

A few seconds later, they were both rushing down the stairs.

"You go look out back," Pappy said. "I'll check out front."

Pappy grabbed his flashlight and opened the door. There was light filtering in from the new, yet to arrive day, but he put the porch light on anyway.

Mockingbirds were singing.

Pappy, his eyes wide and searching, took in the front yard, the orange grove beyond, the grassy lane to the right, and more orange grove beyond that. Then he heard something. Something familiar. He looked down the porch to Buddy's rug, and there he was, curled up and snoring peacefully, and right next to him, snuggled up close, was Milton.

Pappy stared a moment, relief flooding his senses.

Then he quietly closed the door, and shouted through the kitchen, "I found him!" He waited. "Did you hear me?!"

He heard the back door slam and Grandma shouting, "Coming!"

She appeared at the kitchen door. Pappy waved her over.

"You're not gonna believe this."

Grandma looked at him curiously, then he opened the door and pointed.

"Awww," she said. "Will you look at that?"

Then she was gone. A second later, she came back with her camera, focused, and took the shot.

They watched a minute.

"Oh, my Lord," Grandma said. "Do you think that could be why Buddy didn't come home last night? Do you think Buddy knew Milton got out, and he was out looking for him?"

Pappy could only shrug. "Well, he is a good dog."

"Yes, he is," Grandma agreed with a big sigh. "He certainly is."

*   *   *

The aromas of frying bacon and brewing coffee filled the house.

Everyone was in bed still, except for Annie. From her bedroom she had heard Pappy rummaging around the laundry room, calling for Milton. She had gotten up to investigate and had made it there in time to see the wondrous sight of Buddy and Milton all curled up.

"Awwww."

While Grandma was cooking breakfast, and Pappy was speculating on what might have happened over the previous night, Annie had gone out to the barn with Buddy to collect eggs and check on Star and Oke.

A few minutes later, she burst in the door, shouting, "Pappy! Grandma! Oke has a black eye! And it looks like he got out last night! You hear?! Oke was out last night too!"

Grandma looked to Pappy, and said, "You don't think they all three –"

"Hmm," Pappy said with a raised eyebrow.

"And there weren't any eggs! Not one!!"

"Not one?" Pappy said, and he scratched contemplatively at his long, gray beard.

Epilogue

Afternoon, work all done, hot bathtub time.

"Ahhhhhhh!"

Pappy was all settled in. Buddy was laying nearby, watching the house in case there was a chance for food. Pappy was humming the Buddy song as he picked up his encyclopedia, *Vol. 9: Darwin, Charles to Eastern Religion*, and opened it to the marked page.

"Hm, Dakar, let's see: it's the capital and largest city of Senegal, settled around the 15th century, Portuguese established a presence at Cape Verde and used it as a base for the Atlantic slave trade. Hm. France took over in 1677, and Dakar grew into a major regional port of the French colonial empire. In 1902, Dakar replaced Saint-Louis as the capital of French West Africa. Hm," Pappy mumbled. "St. Louis, huh? I think Uncle Kenny has a kid living there – a different St. Louis. Hm. I think he would be my … second cousin? Once removed?"

"Hi, Pappy,"

"Oh, hey, kiddo. What's up?"

"Oh, nothing. Milton is still asleep. He woke up when I came home from school, but he just yawned and yawned and couldn't keep his little eyes open."

"Buddy's not doin' much better," Pappy said, looking over at the big brown dog, splayed across the grassy lawn. His eyes were closed but pointing in the direction of the back porch. "He didn't even want to come with me and Big Red into town when I offered. I opened the door, and he just looked inside, then back at the porch. Why, I've never had to tell him twice to get in Big Red. And when he did, he crawled in there like some old man, taking one step at a time. He slept the whole time we were gone."

"Awww," Annie said. She leaned over to scratch Buddy behind the ears. "Good boy, Buddy."

Buddy didn't move. He barely opened his eyes.

"And look at Oke out there," Pappy said, pointing at the donkey slouching under the oak tree in the pasture. "He hasn't moved since me and Buddy got home today."

"Poor Okey Donkey," Annie sighed. "So, Pappy, do you think they were all together last night? All three of them?"

Pappy shrugged. "Maybe."

"Aunt Cackie said she thinks that when Buddy discovered that Milton had escaped, he and Oke went after him. They probably all three had a big adventure in the forest last night and met all the forest animals."

"Hm," Pappy said, setting Vol. 9 down. "I've gotta tell you, I was thinkin' the same thing."

"Really? The same thing as Aunt Cackie?"

"Mm-hm."

"That's funny," Annie said. "Because Aunt Charlotte always says you and Aunt Cackie think the same." She paused and grinned. "Because you're both kooks."

Pappy smiled. "We are both kooks," he agreed. "But I bet we're right on this one." He looked at Annie, and said, "You do agree, don't you? That those three were out on an adventure last night?"

Annie gave a thoughtful scowl.

Then, with a widening grin, she said, "I sure do, Pappy. I just know it!" She turned to Buddy, and said, "Right, Buddy? You three had a big night out, didn't you?"

Buddy's ears twitched, but not another muscle moved.

Grandfather looked to granddaughter, and he said, "I can certainly see Buddy goin' off to rescue Milton. He is a good boy – and Oke too."

"He sure is, Pappy. Buddy's a good, good boy."

"Yes, he is," Pappy replied. "Even when he's bad, Buddy's good."

"Yep," Annie agreed with a sigh. "Even when Buddy's bad, he's good."

The End.

From, **Gone with the Woof: Bad Dog II,** *by Tim Robinson*

It was war.

This wasn't one of these minor cat-chasing-mouse things you hear about. No, this wasn't even lion chasing antelope. Or even man hunting lion, a struggle in which one party has a distinct advantage over the other. No, this was war. Real war. A contest of equals, the top players in the animal kingdom vying one against the other for ultimate supremacy. Yes, this was war. Real war.

This was Man (and Buddy) vs Armadillo.

Pappy and Buddy stared with consternation down into the hole leading under the back porch.

Hands were set firmly on hips.

Both combatants wore deep, furrowed, contemplative scowls on their faces. In that regard, their faces: one was quite handsome, behind the fright of hard-won years, and wore a long, lustrous, gray beard; the other was handsome as well, with engaging brown eyes and a wide black, attractive muzzle – he wore a naturally philosophical expression.

"Dag-nabbed armadillies."

"Yeah. Dag-nabbed armadillies," Buddy, the big brown dog, agreed.

Of course, if there were no rules to war, it would be fait accompli, for Pappy would have, by now, gone for Old Bessy and scattered a load of yeehaw off the offensive intruder's hard, buckshot-proof hide. Yes, it would have been done and over by now. At the very least, they would have sent him, or her, packing, down the grassy lane, never to return. But, there are rules to war, these days, and the no-shooting rule had been enacted and ratified some time ago by Grandma, the day, in fact, that she had seen a mommy armadillo with her three adorable baby armadillos trailing along behind.

"But," Pappy had resisted. "What if it's a male armadilly? Can I shoot it then?"

The edict had been a resounding no; still, Pappy and Buddy were trying to figure out what this one was. Buddy thought it was a male.

"Are you sure?" Pappy asked.

"No," Buddy replied.

"Maybe you should just go down there and bring him, or her, out," Pappy suggested. "You are the farm dog, you know."

"Uh … no thanks," Buddy replied. "Didn't I hear you telling Grandma that armadillos have leprosy."

"Well," Pappy hemmed. "I didn't say they have leprosy; I said they are known to carry leprosy."

"Well, I don't want to take a chance on that, getting leprosy … whatever that is." Buddy scratched his big head. "What is leprosy, anyway?"

Pappy scratched his long, gray beard. "I'm not sure, really. But you're probably right. You don't want ta be takin' a chance on it."

"Exactly," Buddy agreed. "Anyway, I've already tried picking one up, remember? They just roll into a ball and I can't get my mouth around him – or her."

Pappy studied Buddy's mouth.

"It's not a real long mouth, is it, Budiford? Not a lot of grasping room there."

"Don't reckon so," Buddy replied.

Once again, man and dog stared down into the hole.

"Well," Pappy said, "desperate times call for desperate measures."

"Yep," Buddy agreed. "So what do you got in mind?"

"Only the most desperate of measures, my old pal Budiford. I'm gonna put out some money, that's what."

Buddy's engaging, brown eyes displayed surprise. Shock even.

"Really?"

"That's right. Really. You and me, we're goin' ta town right now, down ta Cousin Travis's, and get us a varmint trap. It's not like I'm bein' impulsive; I've always wanted one. Might use it ta catch us some 'a those durn-testable raccoons that keep comin' around here, causin' all kinds 'a grief for me … and you."

"Durn-testable raccoons," Buddy concurred.

With that, Pappy yelled into the house through the open Dutch door, "Me and Buddy's goin' ta town!"

"All right!" Several voices shouted back from the kitchen. Then, "Oh wait, Pap!"

It was Grandma.

"Could you get these few things down at Uncle Moe's?"

Pappy and Buddy looked at each other, sighed, and turned around for the list.

Buddy waited while Pappy got his list, and his kiss, then they were off.

A minute later they were in Big Red, Pappy's cranky old pick-up truck, driving down the grassy lane, past Star, the giant, useless but beautiful and graceful racehorse, and Okee Donkey – none of those things.

Buddy stuck his head out the window and shouted *adios*.

"Woof!"

Find more of Tim Robinson's books at atroicalfrontier.com or amazon.com/author/timrobinson.

Made in the USA
Columbia, SC
10 June 2022

61566123R00064